MW00587331

Sherlock Holmes
Consulting Detective

AIRSHIP 27 PRODUCTIONS

Sherlock Holmes: Consulting Detective, Vol. 4

The Adventure of the Clockwork Courtesan © 2013 I.A. Watson
The Problem of the Coincidental Glance © 2013 Aaron Smith
The Adventure of the Black Katana © 2013 Bradley H. Sinor
The Adventure of the Anonymous Heiress © 2013 W.R. Thinnes
The Adventure of the Limehouse Werewolf © 2013 Andrew Salmon

Interior llustrations © 2013 Rob Davis
Cover illustration © 2013 Chad Hardin

Editor: Ron Fortier
Associate Editor: Ray Riethmeier
Production and design by Rob Davis.

Published by
Airship 27 Productions
www.airship27.com
www.airship27hangar.com

ISBN-13: 978-0615758237

ISBN-10: 0615758231

All rights reserved under International and Pan-American Copyright
Conventions. No part of this book may be reproduced in any manner without
permission in writing from the copyright holder, except by a reviewer, who
may quote brief passages in a review.

Printed in the United States of America

10 9 8 7 6 5 4 3 2 1

Sherlock Holmes
Consulting Detective
Volume IV

Sherlock Holmes

in

"The Adventure
of the
Clockwork Courtesan"

By
I. A. Watson

*T*he Vienna Automaton was stolen from a customs house at Dover at one fifteen in the morning. A night-watchman surprised the thieves and was beaten within an inch of his life. The robbers came prepared with a heavy wagon and the crated treasure was hoisted aboard and vanished, seemingly without trace.

Sir Harry Wickham, the collector who had bought the piece at auction in Amsterdam, wasted no time in contacting Mr. Sherlock Holmes.

My initial impressions of that case were ones of haste and rapid travel. Summoned from my practice at three a.m. with hardly time to refer my patients to my long-suffering locum, I was bundled aboard an express from Charing Cross; before I had even heard the reason for my sudden departure we were speeding down to the channel port.

Holmes was alert despite the hour, his penetrating stare warning other passengers to stay well clear of him.

"The Vienna Automaton, Watson," he briefed me as the train hurtled through the night. "A marvel of eighteenth century engineering, following on from the works of Pierre Jaquet-Droz. It was the fashion for a while to create lifelike simulacra that moved by clockwork and reproduced human behaviour. Jaquet-Droz and his collaborators created three significant works that yet survive and function: a mechanical woman who actually plays an organ, a mechanical child that can draught four different pictures, two of them said to depict Louis XV and Marie Antoinette, and another that actually writes sentences up to forty characters long[1]. The Vienna Automaton follows from that tradition and is considered a masterpiece of the clockmaker's art. It sold at auction two weeks ago for seven hundred guineas.[2]"

"Am I to understand that this device has been stolen, Holmes?"

Holmes nodded as he packed his pipe. "Within hours of disembarking from the ferry. The whole thing has been planned with an efficiency I find attractive. The thieves knew when and where their target would be. They came prepared and equipped to efficiently extract it despite its bulk and weight. They made good their getaway and the police are, as the news-

---

1 These remarkable toys were produced between 1768 and 1774 by Pierre Jaquet-Droz, his son Henri-Louis Jaquet-Droz, and Jean-Frédéric Leschot to promote the sale of pocketwatches amongst the nobility of Europe. They still exist and work today, displayed at the Musée d'Art et d'Histoire in Neuchâtel, Switzerland.

2 This might equate to around £200,000 or $300,000 in today's currency.

sheets are so fond of saying, baffled. A wonderful problem."

"And so you have been called in to consult on the matter?"

Holmes frowned slightly. "The criminals made one error. Apparently the regular night-watchman was absent due to his child's illness so a substitute took his rounds. This new man's routine was clearly different from the regular guard's circuit and so he stumbled upon the theft and was assailed. I do not yet know what the victim's condition might be."

"But you believe that he may be able to give some testimony that will help to find the culprits?"

"Perhaps later, when and if he awakes. The information telegraphed to me is perforce sketchy, Watson, but I am given to understand that the man is unconscious. However, that disruption seems to have been the only unforeseen event in an otherwise well-planned theft, and disruptions are where we shall find any mistakes our felons might have made."

I was glad to see my friend roused from the ennui that often shrouds him when he lacks an intellectual challenge. We settled in our seats and let the mail train rush us to the docks.

※

Sir Harry Wickham was a civil servant attached to the Foreign Office, a fussy plump man with a thin waxed moustache and a worried frown. He waited at the customs house and was in the courtyard to meet us before we had even alighted from the growler we'd taken from the station.

"Mr Holmes, Dr. Watson, it was good of you to come!"

Holmes returned Sir Harry's handshake perfunctorily. Already his gaze was turning to the service alley where a gate-door had been forced. A pair of uniformed constables now belatedly guarded the entrance.

"How do you do, Sir Harry," I responded, relegated as usual to the task of returning the common courtesies while my friend's remarkable mind raced on other tracks. "I gather it was you who sent the telegram seeking assistance?"

"I am the owner of the stolen automaton," the civil servant agreed. "I am very concerned for her well-being."

"Her well-being?"

"The model is shaped like a beautiful woman, Dr. Watson. It is hard to think of such a work of art as a mere 'it.'"

Holmes ignored the conversation and strode over to examine the open gate-door. He gave the sundered padlock a mere cursory inspection, paused for a moment to check the cobblestones for wheeltracks, then vanished inside the customs shed.

Sir Harry was a portly man who sweated. Concern had made his face red and unhealthy. The civil servant latched onto me to express his losses. "The article in question has quite a history, although no-one is aware of her actual origins[3]. She is often known as the Clockwork Courtesan because she is gowned and jewelled as a high lady of the Chinese court. She sits on a Louis XV chair supporting a small harp on her lap, and when set in motion she plays this instrument while a small caged bird, also of cunning clockwork, dances beside her. The piece was presented at the Austrian court in 1785 to great acclaim. It is extremely valuable and quite irreplaceable."

"Her purchase and transportation to this country would be well reported then?" I surmised.

"In certain circles, yes," agreed Sir Harry. "I gather the bidding was quite vigorous when she was auctioned in the Amsterdam saleroom. Fortunately my agent prevailed and I acquired the piece for my collection." His face fell. "I had acquired her."

"You collect automata?" I enquired.

"I collect clocks," the civil servant told me, "but as a horologist I could hardly ignore so wonderful and significant a piece of clockwork as the Vienna Automaton."

I was keen to find Holmes and see where his investigations had led him. "Perhaps we could discuss this inside?" I suggested to Sir Harry. "We will need more details of your purchase: how your agent shipped the object, what route it took, what precautions were taken for its security, what arrangements were in place for it to be taken from Dover to your home."

Sir Harry assented and we walked towards the gate-door; but just then Holmes strode out, his long coat billowing out behind him. "Come, Watson!" he called. "There is no time to lose. We need to charter a fast train to London!"

"I beg your pardon!" objected Sir Harry. "The investigation…"

"Leads to London, Sir Harry," my friend insisted. "I know now how to find where your Automaton is likely to be taken and time is of the essence. To the station!"

---

3 The makers of several famous automata have been forgotten. One such complicated automaton capable of drawing pictures and writing verses in both English and French was presented to the Franklin Institute in Philadelphia in 1928. Its mysterious origin was solved when the machine was restored to working order and the clockwork figure scribed the words "Written by the automaton of Maillardet," identifying itself as a creation of the Swiss clockmaking Maillardet brothers.

"Come, Watson! There is no time to lose. We need to charter a fast train to London!"

If the name of Mr. Sherlock Holmes did not prompt the London, Chatham, and Dover Railway Company to secure a private train and car for his immediate use, the urgings of Sir Harry Wickham did. The staff at Dover moved with admirable alacrity at odds with the line's usual reputation and we were steaming back to London less than an hour after Holmes had quit the customs house.

"Perhaps now you could explain to us the reasons for this urgent dash?" I asked the great detective once we were settled into our private lounge car. Sir Harry was fit to burst, so it seemed appropriate to win him some exposition. As a medical man I was concerned at his choler.

When Holmes is in full chase his mind runs far ahead of those around him and it is often difficult to convince him to explain for those who cannot match his acuity. I found it fortunate that Holmes was now accustomed to my portuning and willing to explain his reasoning.

"As I told you before, Watson, the best chance of finding a clue to the crime was at the scene of the interruption where the night guard came across the intruders. The burglary had otherwise been well-planned. There are some interesting lines for later investigation, to discover how the thieves knew in good enough time when the Automaton would be unshipping to be able to scout the watchman's routing and to make such diligent preparations. However, the unforeseen accident of a substitute guard with a different routine caused them to diverge from their plan sufficiently to leave a trace."

"What did you find in the warehouse, then that sent us haring back to London like this?" Sir Harry demanded.

"The thieves used a crowbar to break the sturdy McWilliams padlock and backed their dray right up to the doors. The wagon had a wheelbase of seven feet two and a half inches and steel-rimmed wheels with a width of four and a quarter inches. The rear wheels had a circumference of four feet nine, as evidenced by the regularity of an imperfection in one track which left a mark each time it turned. A pair of dray horses had muffles tied to their hooves."

I admitted that this sounded like a professional operation.

"There were five men, although one remained with the dray and kept the horses quiet. Each thief wore new boots, probably intending to discard them after this adventure. They went straight to the rack where the Automaton was crated."

"How could they know where the device would be stored within the warehouse?" I wondered.

"There is only one area suitable for containers of that size," Holmes replied. "The actual crate was numbered and a manifest was readily available on a clipboard hung on the wall. However, the evidence suggests that the robbers must have identified the location of their target earlier in the evening. Another line of enquiry."

"Then why are we leaving such leads behind?" demanded Sir Harry. "I was told that you were thorough and tenacious."

Holmes ignored him. "The thieves knew the crate to be heavy. They used the custom house's own block and tackle to transfer the pallet onto piano wheels they had brought for the purpose. It was at this point that their plan hit the snag."

"The night guard heard them," I guessed.

"The lifting had been timed for the moment when the regular man would have been checking the far sheds," Holmes said. "Thus the noisiest and riskiest part of the operation would have taken place in relative safety. Instead, the substitute guard came upon the felons and challenged them."

"One man against four or five?" Sir Harry frowned.

"His discarded whistle is still lying beneath one of the pallets," Holmes reported. "I surmise that three men were lifting the crate but a fourth was keeping watch from a place of concealment. There is slight evidence that a man in grey gabardine concealed himself in a niche between two piles of boxes. Whatever the case, he had come armed. Judging from the description of the watchman's injuries, he was first stunned with a gat or cosh then generally set upon with fists and boots."

"These men showed no mercy," I shuddered.

"And that was their mistake. In the tussle one of their dark lanterns must have fallen to the floor. The spilled oil pattern is quite distinctive. It must have been extinguished and needed relighting. The thief used this match."

Holmes unwrapped his handkerchief and showed us the charred remains of a small wooden stick.

Sir Harry was unimpressed. "I fail to see why that has sent us racing to London."

"It is a red phosphorous match," Holmes told him impatiently.

Sir Harry looked blank.

"Most matches are dipped in white phosphorous. It is cheap and readily available but can flare unexpectedly and is dangerous for the workers who have to prepare the matches."

"There was a strike about it three years ago," I remembered. "Embarrassing to the prominent liberal, William Bryant, whose match factory was brought to a halt.[4]"

"This match has the distinctive odour of red phosphorous," Sherlock Holmes explained. "It is made of British pine rather than the aspen used by Swiss manufacturers. And just this month a safety-match factory was opened up in Bow by the Salvation Army to provide better conditions for the children used as match-dippers[5]. There are other ways of acquiring their product than from the match-sellers on Bow Street, of course—our criminals might be habitual subscribers to the War Cry[6]—but it is a useful first indicator."

"I still fail to see..." Sir Harry objected, but Holmes cut him short. The detective took a black woolen glove from his pocket and handed it to the civil servant.

"To light the match our felon had to remove his glove," Holmes said. "In the thieves' haste to stick to their schedule he either forgot it or had no time to hunt for it. Turn it inside out."

Sir Harry reluctantly inverted the object and I craned my neck to see what Holmes had spotted. "Coloured thread?" Stitched inside the glove's wrist were strands of red, lilac, and pink cotton.

"A pawnbroker's mark," Holmes supplied. "An identifying mark to prevent shoplifting and to pin together a pair of gloves that might

---

4 In an early act of industrial action, the match girls of London went on strike in July 1888. Initially provoked by the dismissal of one of their number, the girls also protested poor working conditions in the Bryant & May match factory, citing fourteen-hour work days for poor pay, excessive fines, and the severe health risks of working with white phosphorus, such as phossy jaw. Women's rights activist Annie Besant became involved, prominent social reformers of the day set up a strike fund to support the match girls, and the whole affair became a political embarrassment, with debate in the Houses of Parliament. It was also personally embarrassing for factory owners Francis May and William Bryant, both prominent Quakers, who eventually agreed to major reforms of working conditions. Bryant & May switched entirely to using the safer but more expensive red phosphorous matches by 1901. Later health and safety legislation put an end to the manufacture and sale of white phosphorous matches in the United Kingdom.

5 In 1891 the evangelical Christian church movement, the Salvation Army, acted on their concern about child workers handling white phosphorous matches; some children had died. The Salvation Army opened up a safety-match factory using the safer red phosphorus under more carefully regulated conditions. The enterprise struggled, since white phosphorous matches made with lower-paid labour cost far less, but was supported by ethical purchasers and those that valued the superior product. The factory operated until it was bought out by Bryant & May in 1901.

6 The Salvation Army newspaper, which advertised the red phosphorous matches for mail-order.

otherwise be separated."

"Are pawnbroker's colours distinctive, then?" I wondered.

"For the most part," Holmes agreed. "This particular tag is regularly used by one Jimmy Shreeve, who operates an emporium on Maiden Lane… just off Bow Street."

✕

It was still early when we returned to London. Dull grey dawn barely penetrated the dirty air. The first hawkers were beginning to fill the streets but most curtains remained closed. That did not prevent Holmes from hammering on the pawnshop door until Jimmy Shreeve appeared to help with our enquiries.

"Allow us to see your register entry for the sale of this glove and we shall look no further into the others," Holmes told the quivering pawnbrowker. From this I concluded that my friend knew Shreeve to be a petty fence or swindler.

Shreeve was not going to oppose Mr. Sherlock Holmes. He readily turned over his grubby sales ledgers and stood by anxiously, hopping from one leg to another as Holmes turned their pages.

"You sold a load of dark-coloured clothing the day before yesterday, including five pairs of gloves," Holmes noted as he studied, not looking up at the pawnbroker. "To whom did you make that sale?"

Shreeve glanced across at Sir Harry Wickham and me but found no solace. Sir Harry was still red and bristling after the theft. The pawnbroker was compelled to answer. "I don't recall exactly, Mr. Holmes. It were a right busy day, that one, and…."

Now Holmes fixed Shreeve with a gimlet stare.

"It were Flat Mick Woolerton," Shreeve babbled quickly. "Flat Mick as lives off Macklin Street."

Rather unnecessarily Sir Harry removed a slim pocket-book from his jacket and noted down the address. I knew that Holmes would be intimately aware of both man and location.

"And where would Mr. Woolerton have the wherewithal to pay for the garments he purchased with a ten-shilling note?" wondered my friend. The ledgers included the coinage tendered and change rendered.

"I don't know. I didn't ask. That's not my place!" Shreeve stammered. He'd backed away as if Holmes was physically threatening him, until he was pressed up flat against his cluttered shelves of pawned clothing and kitchen items and could retreat no further.

Holmes slammed the account book shut with a bang. "You have been most helpful," he told the pawnbroker.

Shreeve's face paled. "But you won't...."

"I shall omit your assistance from any comment I make to Flat Mick and those who undoubtedly hired him to procure clothing from you."

Shreeve was still stuttering his thanks when we left his shop.

✕

"Who is this 'Flat Mick' person?" demanded Sir Harry Wickham as Holmes strode along Long Acre Street and turned left into Drury Lane.

"A gutter rat," Holmes replied. "One of too many workless men who scrape a living on the edge of the law, surviving on petty thefts and errands between his alcoholic binges. He will not have been involved in the actual theft of your property—the job was too professional for that. His role will have been to purchase the clothing the robbers wore, dark unremarkable clothing that could then be discarded."

"But he can tell us who he bought the clothes for?" I suggested.

"If he still lives, yes."

"And you know where to find this... gutter rat?" Sir Harry asked. "Perhaps we should call a constable to assist us on these rough streets?"

"Watson and I are armed," Sherlock Holmes assured the nervous civil servant. "We will require London's finest later on, but for now we are best unencumbered by representatives of the law."

"We go to the courtyard off Macklin Street?" I checked. "Or will we find Woolerton in some seedy tavern?"

"Let us try his lodgings first," Holmes told us. "It was two days ago when Flat Mick acquired the garments from Jimmy Shreeve. That suggests that he had his fee around that time. He will since have had every opportunity to drink it away and be turned out of the public houses as a pauper again. We can only hope that he had enough foresight to pay his landlady her due before he went to celebrate his earnings."

In the distance the bells chimed seven. "Is our hunt so urgent that we can disturb his landlady's household at breakfast?" I wondered.

"A half-crown from Sir Harry will doubtless quieten her complaints. There are features about this case that concern me and time may be of the essence, Watson."

"You do not think they mean to damage the Courtesan?" worried Sir

Harry. "The value of her component parts is far slighter than her worth as a work of art."

"I do not have the information to draw any conclusion," the great detective told him. "There are enquiries I must put in hand later. For now the trail leads—here!"

Holmes stopped beside a peeling front door in a shabby courtyard. A single gas mantle illuminated the square. No garden graced the enclosed space, only a pile of broken barrels and discarded packing cases. A stray dog fled at our approach.

Holmes tested the door. Upon finding it locked he rapped on it with his walking cane.

On the third such tattoo a light flickered through the cracked, dusty glass above the door. After a sound of drawing bolts, the door opened a fraction. "Who's there?" asked an old woman in a sharp rough voice.

"A man with a silver coin who wants to see Flat Mick Woolerton," answered Sherlock Holmes.

The florin won us easy entry and directions to the attic where Woolerton dozed. Holmes and I burst in on the man as he was trying to pry open a tiny rooflight to make his escape.

Woolerton was even more reluctant to offer names than Shreeve had been.

"You'll speak, by George, or I'll see you flogged!" Sir Harry blustered.

Holmes' speech was quiet and reserved. He squatted down beside the cowering felon and ran his gaze over the grubby, frightened figure.

"You have been in Red Lion Square, I perceive," the detective told Woolerton. I followed Holmes' glance to the man's discarded boots and the ochre clay caught in their worn treads. "Perhaps that was where you dallied with a red-haired woman. You had a fight outside the Crown and Bottle and were thrown to your knees. It may be there that you lost at gaming the remaining fee you had been paid for purchasing clothing for your employers."

Once Holmes had spoken I could follow his methods. He had apprehended the copper strand of hair on Flat Mick's collar, had noted the mud on the man's trousers, had read the truth of the split lip, purpled eye and bruised knuckles, and doubtless much more that eluded me. It was enough that his casual demonstration of his deductive gift terrified and convinced the cowering felon.

"I can't name them! They'll do for me!"

"But I am on their trail," Holmes told him. "You are a poor gambler, but perhaps you would care to calculate the odds of your employers being at liberty to harm you since I am seeking them?"

Flat Mick swallowed hard. "I don't want trouble, Mister 'Olmes. I'm just a poor man makin' my way."

"A man making his way to the gallows!" threatened Sir Harry. "Speak up or I'll...."

Holmes silenced the civil servant with a cold glance. He turned back to the trembling Flat Mick. "Then tell me of the job you did," he offered the felon. "You were tasked with finding clothing. What were you told?"

"I was to get five sets of dark clothes," Flat Mick confessed. "Workmen's trousers, jackets, scarves, balaclavas, gloves...."

"Boots?" Holmes asked.

"No. Not boots."

"A pity. Boot sizes would have been instructive. Still, I measured three of them. Proceed."

"I was just to get them all together, that's all."

"What else were you tasked with?"

Flat Mick stiffened again. "Some... other bits and pieces. Crowbars. Pliers. Rope. Night lanterns."

"Matches?"

"Yes. The good sort. Red 'uns."

Holmes shot me a satisfied look. "What else?" he demanded of Woolerton.

"Nothing else," promised the felon; but he quailed under the gaze of the great detective. "I had to make a payment, but naught else."

"What payment?"

Flat Mick attempted to evade Holmes' stare but it was of no use. "Hire of a stable," he said, surrendering. "'Orses and cart."

Holmes leaned forward eagerly. "What stable?"

"Mister 'Olmes... if I tell you they'll kill me!"

Sherlock Holmes cradled his index fingers and tapped them on his lips. "Flat Mick, my client is a rich man. For the address of that stable he will give you two guineas. The express train to Liverpool departs at 7.56. From Liverpool a man could go anywhere with two guineas in his pocket. What do you say?"

Sir Harry stifled his objection to this offer of largesse. Flat Mick looked from the civil servant to Sherlock Holmes and back again. His face showed his indecision.

"I will know if you are speaking the truth," Holmes warned the felon.

"Two guineas," checked Flat Mick. "Today?"

"If I must," Sir Harry said reluctantly. The fat man didn't like the grubby, cringing weasel.

"It was Nick Claggat's stable, in Oncer Yard," Flat Mick blurted before his courage gave out. "That's where I was sent."

Holmes stepped back. Woolerton grabbed the proffered money from Sir Harry and fled from his attic, leaving everything behind.

"To Oncer Yard?" I asked Holmes.

My friend shook his head. "To Scotland Yard," he replied.

⅜

Oncer Yard was a dingy quadrangle lined with warehouses and storage huts. The great bulk of St. Paul's loomed over the wooden stables that occupied the far side of the cobbled square.

Once the constables had been hidden behind hay bales and a wheel-less cart and inside the smelly stalls of the stable itself, Holmes relaxed enough to admit our questions.

"You truly believe that the thieves will come back here?" Sir Harry demanded of him.

"Nick Claggat's not a man to forgive someone who doesn't return his property." Holmes pointed to the tracks in horse dung spattered across the yard. "The cart that carried away your treasure came from this stable. Doubtless the thieves arranged for changes of horses along the way. They will have returned by a circuitous route to evade searchers, which is why it was so vital for us to reach London by the quickest means possible. If we are fortunate we may catch them unshipping your Clockwork Courtesan before she is even uncrated."

"And we mean to take them as they ride in," I added.

"I hope they will be able to offer some detail about this venture," confessed Holmes. "The robbery was well planned, on accurate and timely intelligence. That suggests the item was stolen to order. We may catch the henchmen that executed the theft and beat the watchman near to death, but I also want the man who gave the commission."

"As do I," agreed Sir Henry wrathfully. "You believe the box may be undisturbed?"

"I will be able to tell once I see it," Holmes said. "Of course, it may have been delivered prior to the cart being returned here."

"Then the thieves will be made to tell us where," the civil servant threatened. His moustache quivered.

Any further conversation was halted by the rumble of a dray approaching. Holmes gestured for us to duck down behind a packing crate.

The gates to Oncer Yard creaked open. Two men moved across the cobbles to slide back the stable doors. Three more rode in on the wagon. Behind them, roped under canvas, was a large box.

Inspector Gregson waited until a man had dropped from the cart to close the yard doors before revealing his warrant-card. "Stand still!" he commanded the thieves. "We are officers of the law!"

"Coppers!" shouted one of the criminals. He reached inside his jacket but was felled by a shot from Gregson's revolver. The man by the gates and one by the stable doors tried to make a run for it. Constables wrestled them to the floor.

The other men raised their hands.

"Jack Carrow, Vance O'Dwyer and their gang," Holmes identified the thieves. "All well deserving of Her Majesty's pleasure[7]. This is a good night's work."

I made my way over to Carrow, who was bleeding profusely from a bullet wound in his upper leg. I improvised a hasty tourniquet although I had my doubts it would work.

Sir Harry ignored the arrest of the criminals and scrambled up onto the cart. "My Automaton!" he cried, tearing away the tarpaulin cover, checking the shipping crate for damage.

Holmes took a moment to examine the box for himself than stalked over to question the captured men.

X

Holmes and I met for lunch at Simpson's two days afterwards. My friend nibbled at his fish with little enthusiasm.

"I do not believe our recent exploit will find its way into your published annals," he told me.

"Why ever not, Holmes?" I asked. I had already begun a draft account of our midnight journey to Dover and back, and of how the stolen artwork had been tracked through London's grimy underworld.

"Because the case remains unsolved, Watson. The property has been returned. The night-guard has awoken and will recover in time. The thieves who perpetrated the crime are charged and incarcerated, save Jack Carrow who died late last night. But there the trail runs cold."

---

7 A common euphemism for a stay in prison.

"O'Dwyer and his band have not revealed their employer?"

"O'Dwyer and his band do not know their employer. They describe an unremarkable man in unremarkable clothes who gave them precise instructions and a detailed plan. It was this man who told them to use Flat Mick Woolerton to acquire clothing from Jimmy Shreeve. It was the stranger who outlined the route they would take with Claggat's cart, and who arranged for substitute horses along the way so the pace could be maintained. It was he who made initial payment to Carrow and had arranged to pick up the Clockwork Courtesan the following day and render the remainder of the fee."

"And you have no lead on who this man may be?"

"He was unremarkable in every way, of average height, brown-haired, of middle age, with no distinctive accent or facial hair," reported Holmes. "Although he paid each man ten pounds before the exploit began it was in coin, not in traceable numbered banknotes. His colleague was equally undistinguished."

"His colleague?"

Holmes pushed aside his fish platter. "Carrow and O'Dwyer were instructed to make one stop on their journey back to London, at a lonely barn at Hollingbourne near Maidstone. There another man with as few distinguishing features had them open the side of the crate so he could inspect the stolen Courtesan. This he did in great detail, even going so far as to check her mechanisms and accoutrements. Upon proclaiming himself satisfied that the item was in proper condition he allowed the thieves to seal the crate again and continue on their way."

"This was a different man to the first?"

"So they say. I theorise that both men were acting on behalf of whomever actually planned this theft."

"You will discover him," I assured my friend.

Holmes frowned. "I find the trail somewhat cold, Watson. I have had no response from Sir Harry's agent in Amsterdam regarding others interested in the Automaton. The barn yielded no clues to the unremarkable man. The testimony of the thieves offers no additional lead. The same attention to detail which characterised the theft characterises the way the path to its planner has been obfuscated. I have not encountered this efficiency of criminal planning except for...."

I knew the reason for his pause. "Your suspect master-criminal? Your sescret Napoleon of Crime"

"Perhaps," allowed Holmes. "The methodologies are similar, and of similar efficacy, but this scheming has a different savour."

"You fear another villain of such perspicacity?"

"My fears…" Holmes breathed. "But come, Watson, you must finish your excellent trout."

X

Mary and I spent a lazy Sunday afternoon catching up on correspondence. She was penning letters to friends in the Raj. I tried to read the papers but was discouraged by accounts of political unrest in the Balkans. The editorial spoke of possible war in the Germanic states and its disastrous consequences for British trade treaties and diplomatic alliances. I found the whole tangle disturbing and depressing.

I laid the broadsheets down and took the time to review my journals and continue my accounts of some of Sherlock Holmes' cases. I had set aside the Clockwork Courtesan for now, discouraged by Holmes' own dissatisfaction with the affair's outcome, disquieted by his unease. I was concentrating on the knotty events at Stamford Bridge[8] when the door-bell jangled.

I heard our maid respond and listened out, wondering if this was some emergency call from one of my patients. Instead the parlour door opened to admit Mr. Sherlock Holmes.

Mary took one look at his face and sighed. She put down her pen and rose. "I shall pack a bag for you, John," she said.

"What is it, Holmes?" I asked.

My friend waited until my wife had left the room then answered. "Sir Harry Wickham has been murdered."

"Murdered?" I echoed.

Holmes nodded. "He is dead. And the principal suspect is his Clockwork Courtesan!"

X

The home of Sir Harry Wickham contained many rare and fascinating treasures but by far the most beautiful was the Clockwork Courtesan.

I had not seen her on the night we had recovered her crate from Oncer Yard. I had been treating the wounded Carrow. Sir Harry had arranged for his box to be removed to safety as soon as he could and had vanished

8 "The Problem at Stamford Bridge," from *Sherlock Holmes: Consulting Detective, Volume 1*

with it.

Thus when Holmes and I first entered Sir Harry's private museum I was convinced for a moment that the Courtesan was flesh and blood, so realistic was her sculpting and so skilful her painting.

The article in question was a statue of a young Chinese woman, her porcelain face moulded to resemble some high Asiatic lady, reproducing in every detail the shape, colour, and texture of flesh. She sat on a cushioned chair cradling a golden harp upon her lap. Her eyes were bright and shining, a rare cobalt blue. Her hair, eyebrows, and even her lashes were of genuine hair, midnight black and lustrous. The spots of rouge on her cheeks and lips, the shading tint on her eyebrows, the way the light caught her sculpted cheekbones, all gave her the very semblance of life.

For a heartbeat I was a young man again, far from home in Tientsin, taking in the sights and sounds of that exotic land as only a young man can.

"Did the ladies of Nankai[9] wear such exotic robes, Watson?" my friend Mr. Sherlock Holmes asked me.

I snapped out of my reverie. "How could you possibly know I was thinking of Tientsin?" I demanded.

Holmes snorted. "Your attention was fixed upon the remarkable clockwork object before us, which depicts a geisha or court lady of the last century in hand-made silk robes of the period. However, your eyes were unfocussed and your stance that of a man far from his current surroundings. Furthermore, your hand strayed to your watchchain upon which you habitually retain a five wen coin from your travels as a young man. After those observations, and with the additional advantage of knowing your background and character, the rest was simple."

Inspector Lestrade cleared his throat to remind us that there was serious business at hand. I tore my gaze away from the automaton and dutifully directed it at the rumpled and bloodstained Turkish rug and overturned chair at the far end of the room.

Holmes frowned. "There has been much disturbance here."

Lestrade nodded and held his hands up placatingly. "That was before Scotland Yard was ever called in. When Sir Harry's servants had to force the door to get in they found him bleeding on the floor, his throat gashed. They were unable to lift him due to his significant bulk and so dragged him on the rug to move him towards the window where they could inspect his wounds."

Holmes held his hand up to cut short Lestrade's account. He gestured

9 Tientsin, modern day Tianjin, is in the Nankai Province of China.

for me to inspect parts of the polished parquet floor with him. "The rug was originally positioned here, Watson, beside his desk. Sir Harry was sitting in his chair here behind the desk, facing towards the window when his throat was gashed."

"How...?" began Lestrade.

"My usual methods," Holmes said dismissively. "See the spray pattern of the ruptured blood vessels and the distance the fluid pumped. Observe the splash marks. Consider the different stains where blood has soaked through fabric and where it has pooled unhindered. Sir Harry must have died in his chair then slumped down onto the rug. There he laid for some time before being discovered, bleeding his last, unable to rise or call for help."

He moved on, ignoring the condition his trouser knees were getting in as he crawled the gory floor. "And look here. These smears denote the carpet being dragged with a weight upon it over towards the French window."

"That's what I said," Lestrade objected, unhappy at being cut off.

"First hand evidence is always to be preferred to second hand accounts," Holmes told him.

Lestrade perched his hands on his hips. "Then perhaps you'd be able to tell me what happened after and before, Mr. Sherlock Holmes?" the inspector challenged. "How is it possible that...."

It was time for me to intervene. "Inspector, your constables interrupted a pleasant afternoon and cancelled a most congenial dinner to bring us all the way out to Flaxenridge, but could tell us very little except that Sir Harry Wickham had been found murdered in his home. Perhaps while Holmes is undertaking his first-hand studies you might favour me with some background as to the nature of the tragedy?"

Lestrade pointedly turned his back on the detective shuffling over the floor and addressed himself to me. "Well, doctor, it seems that Sir Harry left his London office at seven last night and rode straight out here to his country seat. He dined alone—there are no guests in the house and no visitors called—then retired early with boxes of paperwork he'd brought with him. This morning after breakfast he retreated to his museum study, this room in which we now stand. That was his custom when he had work to do."

"Where are the papers that were spread out on this writing desk?" Holmes enquired.

"They have been removed for safe keeping by Sir Harry's man of business," Lestrade replied. "There were government documents of a sensitive nature amongst them." He turned back to me, then paused as a thought struck him. "How did Holmes know...?"

"Position of pen and inkpot, the blotter at some distance from the pile of fresh writing paper laid out here, there were clearly other items on the desk to account for the otherwise odd spacing," my friend replied absently. His gimlet gaze flicked over the arrangement of the desk: the empty filing spike, the inkwell and blotter, the envelope rack, the silver tray with the empty china teacup on it, and the sinister dried peripheral blood splatters on one corner. "Sir Harry sat here, writing with this fountain pen that has rolled beneath his desk. He was most probably annotating the papers you have sequestered rather than a new document, for the impressions on the top blank sheet suggest the last note-page written upon was a message to Sir Harry's tailor over a week ago."

"It was a long journey from London," I explained to Lestrade. "Holmes is feeling restless."

The Scotland Yard detective sighed in agreement and continued his account. "At around ten thirty-five this morning a gardener's boy tending the flowerbeds beyond the terrace passed by to refill his watering can and noticed Sir Harry lying on the floor in the middle of the room. It was clear from the blood that Sir Harry was injured. The gardener called the alarm and he, the butler and the footman forced the locked door."

"Was no spare key to be found?" I wondered.

"Sir Harry's key was in the door so no duplicate would have been effective."

I saw the problem. "The door was locked from the inside and the French windows were sealed? I see no other way for a murderer to get out."

Lestrade nodded as I got the salient point. "The French windows are not only screwed shut but painted over. This room contains Sir Harry's valuable clock collection and other rare items of substantial worth. I considered the chimney...."

"The murderer would have had to bring a sweep with him to clean up the soot if that means of access had been used," Holmes scorned. As he spoke he was actually in the fireplace, focussing his magnifying lens on some burned ashes in the grate.

"I considered the chimney and dismissed it as impractical," Lestrade completed his sentence.

"There is a considerable amount of blood," I noted. The body had been removed from the scene so I asked the Inspector, "How did Sir Harry die?

Holmes mentioned a slashed throat?"

"His throat was cut," answered Holmes without looking up from his examination. "A single sharp slice from left to right whilst he sat with his chair swivelled away from his desk. The bloodstains are definitive."

"His throat was cut," agreed Lestrade, frowning unhappily at my friend's omniscience. "But explain this if you can, Mr. Sherlock Holmes."

He pointed to the Clockwork Courtesan. She sat immobile but perfect with her harp and her little caged bird; but in her exquisite white hand the sharp metal edge of her fan was stained with blood.

The Vienna Automaton moved. First she raised her head, twisting it slightly as she shifted. Her blue eyes blinked. Her bosom rose and fell as if she breathed.

Then her hand lifted. To her left the tiny green-plumed mechanical bird slid along its perch inside its golden cage. The peacock fan in her fingers closed—the fan that was still reddened by Sir Henry's lifeblood. The Clockwork Courtesan blinked again and used the base of the fan as a plectrum on the strings of the small harp she held in her lap. She strummed her instrument offering a melodious opening chord.

"Remarkable!" I exclaimed, enchanted. Holmes watched intently. Even Lestrade had fallen silent.

The Courtesan began to play the first movement of Beethoven's Sonata Pathétique[10]. Every note was perfect.

We all watched and listened, rapt, as the beautiful simulacrum performed. Her hand moved so deftly it was hard to believe this was only a machine. The tiny bird hopped upon its perch, varying its motion in sequence with the music. Only when the player's last chord was done and she whirred back to the position from which she had started was the spell broken.

"A masterpiece of the clockmaker's art," admitted Holmes reverently. His awe did not prevent him from lifting the automaton's Chinese skirt to examine the bellows and gears beneath the hooped silk.

"Could she have gashed Sir Harry's throat?" wondered Lestrade. "An accident, perhaps? Or a deliberate trap?"

"You believe this mechanical lady rose from her chair, stalked over to Sir

---

10 Ludwig van Beethoven's Piano Sonata No. 8 in C minor, Op. 13, published in 1799, must have been adapted for the Automaton's instrument.

Harry at his writing desk, then gashed his neck?" Holmes asked scornfully, his hinder parts protruding from beneath the Courtesan's petticoats.

I could see no way that the Vienna Automaton's movements might have inadvertently killed a man, even had he been standing over her; nor how the mechanism's limited range of movement could have allowed it to so accurately slice a throat. Yet there was something disquieting in those china-blue glass eyes as if the high Asian lady kept a sinister secret from us all.

Holmes opened a panel at the back of the Louis Quinze chair upon which the clockwork damsel sat. Inside was a key-wheel to wind the device and a slotted drawer. The compartment contained eight iron cylinders the length of my hand, with strange perforations in them, and one empty space. A ninth such cylinder resided in a complicated mechanism of springs, hammers, and gears.

"This is her clockwork brain!" Holmes exclaimed. "See, Watson, Lestrade! Each of these cylinders can fit into the mechanism. As the coil rotates the cylinder, the bumps and holes on the tube's surface raise and lower those hammers that trail across it. The hammers' movements control the gears and rods that determine the mannequin's motion."

"And each of these tubes has her play a different tune!" I realised, reading the titles engraved upon each cylinder.

"Indeed, Watson. And with each, a slightly different set of movements. We must try each one to ensure that no range of action might have allowed Sir Harry's death."

I wondered whether Holmes was merely being thorough in eliminating the impossible or whether he wished to hear again the music of the Clockwork Courtesan.

Holmes questioned the household:

"Sir Harry was a man of fixed habits at home," Baxter the butler told us. "Since Lady Elizabeth's death he retires early after a light supper. He rises around seven, takes a short walk around the garden, then takes breakfast in the white drawing room. If he has boxes from the ministry he goes into his museum where he keeps his work-desk. He is not to be disturbed there except for a cup of Darjeeling at 9:15 and at 11:15 a.m. He will generally finish work around noon and expect lunch at one." The man's face fell. "Or at least he did."

"Was it usual for him to lock himself into his museum whilst he worked,"

"We must try each one to ensure that no range of action might have allowed Sir Harry's death."

Holmes enquired.

"Very unusual, sir. The museum was generally locked when he was not present, because of the value of the collection; but Sir Harry did not lock himself in. We knew he was not to be interrupted. It would have disturbed him to have to get up and let the maid in to serve his morning tea and his elevenses."

"Did Sir Harry mention any particular work he was undertaking this morning?"

"Not that I recall, sir. He had three red boxes with him from the ministry, which is a heavier load than usual, but not unheard of."

"Did he send any messages or letters?"

"He would usually pass them to Milly when she served his tea."

※

"I was filling the watering can for Mr. Blakeney," the gardener's boy testified. He was a gangling youth of thirteen or so who would soon be too old for this kind of service. His face was a rash of acne made worse by his blushes at the attention to his tale. "The quickest way is through the small garden by the museum to the old pump behind the outhouse privy. That's why I was going past the window."

"Why did you peer into the room?" interrogated Holmes.

The boy flushed redder yet. "I heard her, sir. That mechanical lady. I heard her making her music."

Holmes' eyes narrowed. "She was playing?"

"Aye, sir. Beautiful music, it was. Both times. I... I looked in to see her moving."

"Both times?" Holmes queried.

The boy stumbled on with his explanation. He had been sent for water twice, once around nine-thirty and again at the time he discovered the death. On both occasions the Courtesan had been playing. "She was doing this lovely tune, sirs. I had to stop and listen."

"And then you saw Sir Harry," I prompted.

The boy shuddered. "That second time he was lying on the mat at her feet, lying on his belly. At first I thought he'd just fallen but then I saw the red on the rug. I ran to get..."

"In a moment," Holmes interrupted. "The first time you peered in, what was Sir Harry doing?"

"Why, he was watching her, too!" the gardener's lad exclaimed. "He was listening while he was jotting something down in his book."

"Now describe the murder scene more, that second occasion. Was the automaton still moving? What was the position of Sir Harry's body? Was the blood still liquid?"

The gardener's lad proved a most unsatisfactory witness. When he'd seen the blood he had completely lost his head and fled to tell Mr. Blakeney, the head gardener. Under Holmes' impatient questioning we eventually learned that Sir Harry lay on the floor beside his desk as if he'd toppled from his chair. His head was turned from the window. The blood on the rug had spread to the full extent to which it was now stained. The boy did not remember whether the courtesan had moved. He offered no other help.

"I was there when we burst the door in," Mr. Blakeney reported. "Soon as I saw the boy was serious, I warned Mr. Baxter and we went to master. We was surprised to find the door fastened against us. It took three of us, me, Mr. Baxter and Hockney the footman, to break it down. That room's well secured, with heavy leads in the windows and a good strong lock."

"What did you observe in the room?" demanded Holmes.

"Master was laid face down in a pool o' drying blood. Sticky it was, but not runny. His throat had been cut, that much was clear when we turned him over if it hadn't been from the gore right across the carpet. We dragged him to the window to see if aught could be done for him but it were too late."

"What happened then?"

"Mr Baxter sent Hockney for the police and for Mr. Eddington—that's Sir Harry's man of business. Me and Mr. Baxter looked around the room, like, because it was clear it was murder. He opened the cupboard doors and I stood ready with my shovel. But there was nobody in none of them. So I went to quiet down the boy since he was near hysterical and Mr. Baxter gave order that nobody was to go into the museum until the Peelers arrived."

Milly the maid had been weeping. Her eyes were reddened and she sniffed into a sodden lace hanky. "You must be brave now and tell us what you can about this terrible affair, my dear," I told her.

The maid outlined her regular routine, how she brought her employer refreshment twice during his morning's work. On the day of his murder she had served his 9:15 am tea as normal then returned to the kitchens. The museum door had not then been locked. She had received no letters to post that day.

"What was Sir Harry doing when you took him his tea?" Holmes interrogated.

"He had that mechanical girl playing, sirs. That Chinese lady. She was strumming on her harp real beautiful. Master must have really liked that music 'cause he was playing it all morning." She hummed a few off-key bars.

Holmes had no interest in literature or art but his regard for music was keen. "Mozart's Piano Concerto No. 27 in B flat major," he identified. His eyes narrowed. "Just that one piece or all of them?"

"Just that one bit o' music, sirs. I can hear it in my head even now. Gives me the shudders to remember it, though."

X

Sir Harry Wickham's man of business was a dapper youngster in an expensive morning suit.

"You arrived shortly after the police," Holmes checked with Mr. Eddington.

The man of business confirmed this. "It was a terrible shock. Fortunately Sir Harry had long since furnished me with clear instructions on what to do in the case of his demise."

"What were they, pray?"

"Well, apart from the usual matter of recording the death and following the will through probate and so on, I was to immediately telegram his ministry to alert them of his passing. I was to seal any red boxes he might have with him and await their collection by government courier. I was to inform his closest kin, an older brother in Edinburgh and a niece in Bath, and his Club."

"Who inherits?" I wondered.

"That is no secret. His estate goes to his brother, with a series of bequests to family, friends, and retainers."

"Sir Harry must have had considerable wealth to accumulate so great a clock collection," I imagined.

"He was a shrewd investor," agreed Eddington.

"He paid a significant sum for his final acquisition," noted Holmes. "I understand the auction was in Amsterdam. What arrangement did he make to bid there?"

"I engaged the services of a local agent. Mr. Van Droot has made purchases for Sir Harry before. He was given a limit of eight hundred guineas but fortunately was able to acquire the piece for less than that sum."

"There were other bidders, however."

"Indeed. Bidding was quite fierce until it became clear that Van Droot was determined to acquire the piece."

"Who made the arrangements for shipping?"

"Van Droot's office handled transportation to Dover. I arranged for the item's pick-up once it cleared customs. Stanning and Sons is a local Staffordshire haulage firm that we have used before."

I stifled a sigh. With so many aware of the transportation of the automaton it would be near to impossible to discover how word of its arrival reached the thieves.

"Stannings brought the item here when it was recovered from London," added Eddington.

Holmes also questioned the man of business on Sir Harry's civil service work.

"I knew little about that," Eddington confessed. "Sir Harry kept his personal business and his ministry affairs properly separate. I know he divided his time between the Foreign Service and the War Office, although more at the former. For more on that you must speak to his government staff."

X

Finally Holmes spoke to Inspector Lestrade himself. "I suppose you have already solved the case," the policeman predicted gloomily. "Who is it you want me to arrest?"

"I have not unravelled this affair," Sherlock Holmes told him. "Not by a long way yet. I have calls to make and telegrams to send. I must speak again with the gardener's boy and seek out the coroner then travel back to London by the next train."

"Then what shall I tell my superiors?" asked the inspector.

"Tell them that you are paying special attention to the iron cylinders of the Vienna Automaton," Holmes advised him. "Tell them that you are looking for whatever was on the scraps of burned paper in Sir Harry's museum fireplace. Tell them you seek a small man, or possibly a lithe woman, no more than five foot two, who might have been seen leaving the vicinity this morning. He or she may be left-handed. Tell them that you are especially interested in the notches on the clockwork bird's perch. Detain the household staff for further questioning. And report that Sir Harry was already drugged to unconsciousness at the time his throat was opened. That should keep your superiors quiet."

He stalked from the room before Lestrade lifted his dropped jaw.

The local coroner's office was a small room in the cottage hospital. As we waited for Dr. Greenaway to return from his rounds, Holmes looked at me with a wry amusement. "Ask your questions, my friend, before you explode," he advised.

"I confess to some curiosity," I admitted. "Those things you said to Lestrade...."

"Mere trifles, Watson. Initial observations. There is more to this than the blatantly obvious."

"I would still appreciate some exposition, Holmes. What led you to your conclusions?"

My friend shook his head sadly. "Everything was plainly there for any observer to see. Sir Harry's throat was cut yet there was no sign of a struggle. Save for his fountain pen on the floor, the contents of his desk were undisturbed. A thrashing, flailing man trying to save his life would have swept boxes and envelopes all across the room. Doubtless when the dregs of Sir Harry's teacup are subjected to forensic analysis, the chemists will confirm the bitter aroma in the lees as henbane."

"A notorious sedative," I noted.

"Indeed. And one that may implicate one or more of the household staff. The substance must have been introduced to the tea-caddy or the teapot before Sir Harry was served his first refreshment in his museum study."

"And the rest? The scraps of burned paper? The clockwork bird's perch? The small left-handed man or woman?"

"My dear Watson, when a man burns papers in an otherwise clean hearth just before his demise it is always suggestive. In this case I believe he was noting the movements of the mechanical bird as it danced along to Mozart. The left-handed murderer is indicated—but not conclusively so—from the pattern of blood-spray that denotes the direction of the gash which ended Sir Harry's life. That the murderer stood behind his already-unconscious victim is self-evident."

"The blood sprayed forwards yet the villain left no bloody footprints or other marks. He avoided the effusion."

"Exactly. Furthermore…."

Our conversation was interrupted by the arrival of Dr. Greenaway. Holmes introduced himself and gained us admittance to the dead man's corpse and personal effects.

Holmes did not take long. "A couple of points of interest," he lectured the coroner. "An autopsy examination will confirm the use of Hyoscyamus niger[11] on Sir Harry, leaving him helpless for easy murder. And Sir Harry's personal effects no longer include the pocketbook he was wont to carry, the one Watson and I saw him use on the night the Vienna Automaton was recovered. Since Sir Harry did not use his writing paper but still had draft notes to burn in his hearth they most likely came from that missing journal. It is likely that the murderer stole it."

As I trailed after Holmes back to our hansom to the railway station I pressed him for more information. "I'm still puzzled as to how the killer got into and out of a locked room with the key still in the keyhole," I admitted.

"Then also ask yourself this, Watson. If Sir Harry was drugged and insensible and then lay dead on the rug long enough for the blood to coagulate, why was the Clockwork Courtesan still playing her two-minute music when the gardener's boy looked in?"

I confessed that I had overlooked that point.

Holmes shook his head ruefully. "That is not your only omission, my dear Watson. You will recall that when we tried the Automaton, she played us Beethoven. Yet the serving girl's ill-tuned testimony suggests that Sir Harry was listening to Mozart all morning."

"The cylinders were changed!"

"Indeed they were. And consider this: Sir Harry's account of the Automaton indicated that she was a novelty at the Austrian court in 1785. Yet this morning she was playing Mozart's Piano Concerto No. 27 in B flat

---

11 Commonly called henbane or stinking nightshade, this common European plant was often prescribed for anaesthetic purposes. It is also an hallucinogen. It is fatal in more concentrated doses, but has limited application as a poison because of its distinctive and unpleasant flavour.

major—a work which I recall was completed by Mozart in 1791.[12]"

This seemed odd. "Perhaps an additional cylinder was added later?" I speculated.

"Obviously so," Holmes agreed. "But you might also observe that of the nine cylinders we examined and played today, Mozart's No. 27 was not amongst them."

Ж

The Strangers' Room of the Diogenes Club was dour and oppressive. Its darkwood walls and heavy plaster mouldings were accentuated by bulky Chesterfields, mahogany tables, and a grey and black Axminster carpet. No wonder that Holmes and I were the only visitors to that august establishment.

I had met the middle Holmes brother on only a few occasions[13]. The family resemblance was easy to see, although Sherlock's sharp, gaunt features were translated in Mycroft into rounded jowls and beady eyes.

"Sherlock, Dr. Watson," he greeted us as he strode into the Strangers' Room like a ship docking in harbour. He lowered his bulk into one of the great armchairs and waited until a steward brought him a drink. "You have recently returned from Staffordshire, I see. How fares your investigation into Sir Harry's sudden demise?"

I could see no route by which Mycroft Holmes might have perceived our recent travel. Both his brother and I had changed from country to city attire. Yet I had heard Sherlock Holmes owning that his older sibling had deductive powers acute as his own, or more, albeit without the practical application to which my friend had placed his abilities.

"You are aware of the circumstances of Sir Harry's death," Sherlock Holmes said. "What can you tell me of the work that Sir Harry was undertaking?"

Mycroft Holmes claimed to hold a minor functionary position within

---

12 Holmes' dating of the work was taken from the date on Mozart's manuscript, 5th January 1791. This was the conventional view at his time for the dating of this piece, and has only been challenged in recent years with forensic evidence suggesting possible composition as early as 1787.

13 The existence of a third Holmes brother has been inferred by Holmesians because of Sherlock's description of his family as "country squires." Since Mycroft occupies a civil service position more likely for a second son, William S. Baring Gould decided in his famous Holmes biography that there must be an older brother who inherited the family's estates and honours. He named him Sherringford, an early draft name for the Great Detective himself from Conan Doyle's notes.

Her Majesty's government. Sherlock Holmes had once told me differently: "He *is* the government, Watson."

Mycroft shifted his bulk. He lived a sedentary life and did not exercise. "As you have already surmised, Sir Harry worked with sensitive information within the Foreign and War Offices, acting as an interface between those departments. His role was to handle and sometimes to interpret information of middling sensitivity."

"He did not strike me as a particularly sensitive analyst," commented Sherlock.

"That is why his workload was only of middling sensitivity," replied Mycroft.

"Was there anything in his official boxes or stored at his house which was worth killing him for?"

"Evidently so. I cannot say what."

Sherlock Holmes regarded his brother for a moment. "How did Sir Harry finance his clock collection?" he asked at last.

"It is said that he was a shrewd investor in stocks and shares," Mycroft replied.

"I mean, did he make his overseas purchases on a budget from the British government or some foreign one?" my friend said bluntly. "I have inspected his accounts. They show no great financial acumen. I can discover where his money came from eventually, but I have no wish to expose the careful precautions of my own nation's security services."

He left the possibility dangling there while Mycroft sipped his drink. At last the government man replied. "On occasion it has been helpful to bring information from another country to our own inside timepieces that Sir Harry has purchased. He was more than happy to indulge his hobby. His superiors were pleased to find ways of evading the attention of alien powers whose objectives and ethics do not accord with ours. But Sherlock, these are matters of state. I cannot assist with your enquiries."

Holmes watched Mycroft. I was struck for a moment by the similarity of their eyes. "I have other investigations to make," my friend said at last. "I shall return later."

"Undoubtedly," replied Mycroft, and returned to his work.

Sydney Melish's Greenwich townhouse had a pleasant prospect over the royal observatory park. I said as much as I settled into his drawing room and accepted a cup of tea from his housemaid.

"You did not come to compliment me upon the view from my windows," old Melish told me, dropping three lumps of white sugar into his own cup. "I read the Telegraph. I am aware of Sir Harry Wickham's demise."

"Then you will understand why your insights and information might be useful," I suggested.

"Useful to your friend Mr. Sherlock Holmes?" Melish asked between sips of his beverage. "I have also read your accounts, Dr. Watson, and some of your friend's monographs. His study on discerning the age of chemical dyes was particularly useful to me once in disproving the provenance of an item I was offered for my collection."

Melish was a collector, too. His house was also filled with clocks.

"Your man in Amsterdam sought to purchase the Vienna Automaton at auction recently," I noted. "Holmes and I hoped you could tell us more about the piece and the circumstances of its sale."

"That is why I expected another visit," the old man said. "What do you wish to know?"

"Another visit?"

Melish sipped his tea, grimaced, and added another sugar cube. "I received another caller on this matter two days ago. That would be the morning after your spectacular recovery of the stolen courtesan, yes? She, too, wanted my expert knowledge of the Automaton, its history and function."

I wished then that Holmes had been present at my interview with Melish, but my friend had garbed himself in the clothes of a street-labourer and hared off who knows where with those young street-arabs he likes to call his Baker Street Irregulars. I had to do my best.

"Perhaps you could tell me about your visitor? What name did she give? What did she look like? What did she ask?"

Melish was amused by my eager questions. "So there is a mystery," he gloated. "How splendid."

"A man has died," I reminded him. "Tell me about your visitor."

Melish rang for a footman, who was able to produce a calling card bearing the name Mrs. Aaron Sylvester and the address 16 North Alderley Street. "She was a lady, well-dressed and well-spoken," the collector recalled. "She represented herself as speaking for Lloyd's of London, the company that had insured the Vienna Automaton. She referred to the tale that morning's papers were bearing about its theft and recovery. She sought general background information on the piece."

I pressed Melish for details of the woman's appearance. My heart skipped as he described an attractive dark-haired young woman of slight build.

Melish told me what he'd told his mysterious caller. "I outlined what I knew of the history of the Clockwork Courtesan for Mrs. Sylvester. The Automaton was presented in the Austrian court in 1785, when the craze for such pieces was sweeping the elite of Europe. Unlike her more famous Swiss and French brothers and sisters, her manufacturer was not identified. She was given as a gift to Lady Elizabet Meissnitzer, then passed in her family until she was sold as an 1822 estate sale lot to M. Cadillet. Thereafter she moved through a series of hands until she was acquired by Major von Rautenstrauch for his own collection. Von Rautenstrauch's recent bankruptcy placed the piece back on the market last year. Her anonymous purchaser sent her to auction again last month and made a reasonable profit on his investment."

"So her most recent previous owner remains unknown?"

"This is not uncommon in the art world. The auction house is a reputable one and the Automaton's provenance was well established, so there was no problem with the sale."

"Apart from yourself and Sir Harry, who else made the bidding?"

"It was reported to me that a representative of Count Maillard made offers. Herr Wertham was also present but dropped out early when it became clear that Sir Harry's man was determined to take the piece. The stiffest competition came from the Italian Bergamasco, who is known to favour such novelty items."

"Might any of these men be willing to pay for the Courtesan to be stolen?"

"Who knows what a collector will do?" shrugged Melish. "It is not very long since your friend exposed the illegal behaviour of Mr. Hector Dorner[14], is it?"

"What else did Mrs. Sylvester ask about?" I wondered.

"She wanted details of the mechanism by which the Courtesan moved. Perhaps you are familiar with the way in which a series of indented iron cylinders operate the pistons that shift the dummy? A similar method is used today to operate the fairground calliopes with their clockwork orchestras, except that there it is perforated cardboard sheets which control the sound and movement of the apparatus."

Holmes had instructed me to enquire about the cylinders that

---

14 As recounted in "Dead Man's Manuscript" in *Sherlock Holmes: Consulting Detective*, Volume 1

controlled the Automaton's mechanism. Melish produced the auction catalogue which described the nine pieces which the Courtesan could play; Mozart was not amongst them. I asked a number of supplementary questions but Melish had nothing else of relevance to tell me. I thanked him for his time and returned to 221B Baker Street.

I was careful to watch for diminutive ladies on my journey home.

Suffice it to say that no Mrs. Aaron Sylvester abided in North Alderley Street.

It was almost morning before Sherlock Holmes reappeared, soaked to the skin and roaring for warm soup from his landlady. He was no longer clad as a labourer but instead peeled off the sopping evening garb of a man about town.

He was comfortably wrapped in his familiar smoking jacket and sucking on a pipe of shag when the long-suffering Mrs. Hudson produced the required sustenance and he felt ready to answer my questions.

"What have you been up to, Holmes?" I demanded.

"I have been chasing phantoms, Watson," came the reply. "The original theft of the Automaton becomes more and more mysterious. It was obviously stolen to order, yet I can find no trail for these undistinguished intermediaries. Nor can my Irregulars find any arrangement to retrieve the crate from the stables as the thieves believed would happen."

"You said that this robbery was well planned."

"But I now believe that the planner never intended to receive the Automaton after its theft. I have also been examining the financial matters of Sir Harry Wickham and Mr. J. E. Eddington. I remain unenlightened as to how a civil servant on a fixed salary with a middling portfolio of investments might acquire so lavish a horological collection."

"You suspect Sir Harry was doing something unscrupulous?"

Holmes spread his fingers to indicate that my guess was as good as his. "My final visit was to some… gentlemen who keep track of various specialists that come into our country to carry out their business; people who prefer to enter and leave our nation without passing through our customs houses or producing passports and travel papers."

"You have been talking to smugglers," I surmised.

"A conversation that ended when I elected to hurl myself into the Thames rather than continue the encounter in the way they would have preferred," Holmes told me with a wry expression. "There alone I have made a breakthrough. A young woman arrived three days since on a merchant ship from the Hook of Holland, paying in silver guilders, using the name Richtenhaus and expecting anonymity."

"A diminutive beauty with dark hair?" I ventured.

Holmes started at me then burst out laughing. "My dear Watson, you are a marvel! Here I am drivelling on about smugglers and bank transfers and you have a story to tell! Never mind my dreary peregrinations. Tell me what you know!"

Despite his late night Holmes was up before me the following morning. I had slept over at my old Baker Street rooms rather than disturb Mary with a late return and was enjoying Mrs. Hudson's kedgeree as my friend made his usual mess clipping items from the morning's papers.

I glanced across to see what had caught his attention. He had cut out a pair of foreign obituaries and an article about the Balkan situation. "Have you moved on from the problem of the Clockwork Courtesan?" I asked him.

His hawk-like face appeared over the newspaper and he shook his head. "Hardly, Watson. I am now gathering the final pieces of the puzzle. When Inspector Lestrade arrives he will doubtless bring the last information I require." He allowed himself a small satisfied smile as the bell rang. "That will be him now."

A few moments later the sly-looking little detective inspector slouched into the room bearing a thick packet of papers. I pushed the toast-rack over to him.

"You have the testimonies?" Holmes demanded of the Scotland Yard man.

Even without the deductive powers of the Great Detective, I could tell from Lestrade's crumpled appearance and baggy eyes that he had enjoyed little sleep. "I've got 'em," he said. "You were right, of course. After the discovery of Sir Harry's body, only Eddington was alone in the room, gathering and sealing papers to send back to the ministry. And there was a lady went into the local post office about the time the murder was discovered. I've got the transcript of the telegram she sent overseas."

Holmes accepted the documents from the inspector as Lestrade helped himself to a generous slab of butter for his toast. I glanced at the telegram but could read only a jumble of seemingly-random letters.

"I reckon that's a code," said Lestrade, redundantly.

"Probably a Playfair cypher," noted Holmes. He sounded indifferent, more interested in browsing the additional statements of the house staff. "Charles Wheatstone's digraph substitution cypher[15], wherein a pair of letters are exchanged for others in a five by five alphabetical matrix."

"Can you crack this, Holmes?" I wondered.

"Given sufficient time, anyone might," he sniffed. "What it says does not matter now."

Lestrade and I both protested that the information might be key to solving the murder of Sir Harry Wickham. Holmes laid down the Inspector's dossier, swept aside the breakfast things, and reached for his cane. "The murder is already solved, gentlemen," he assured us. "Now we must return to Flaxenridge and have the Courtesan catch her for us!"

Jerome Eddington was working at Sir Harry's desk in the museum when Baxter showed us in. The man of business looked up from closing his former employer's accounts with a mild curiosity. "What brings you back here, Inspector?"

Milly trailed behind us carrying a silver tray with crockery on it. I recognised the very tea-set that had been used to deliver the narcotic drug to the murdered householder.

"We have an important point to check, Mr. Eddington," the rat-faced policeman answered. "There is information we have failed to examine."

"We have come to clear this Clockwork Courtesan of the crime of which she has been accused," I said. "Holmes suspects another lady."

Eddington laid down his pen. "Wait! Sir Harry's murderer was female? I don't understand."

Holmes ignored the discussion and immediately threw up the Chinese

---

15 The Playfair square, named after Lord Playfair who popularised its use, was first invented by Charles Wheatstone in 1854. Because it encodes pairs of letters from a 5x5 matrix determined by a keyword rather than using a simple substitution system such as A = B, there are 600 possible letter variations rather than 26, making it considerably harder to crack and nearly impossible with short samples of text. The British Foreign Office declined to adopt the Playfair cypher as standard encryption despite Wheatstone arguing that he could teach "three out of four schoolboys to use it in fifteen minutes." The Under Secretary of the Foreign Office replied, "That is very possible, but you could never teach it to attachés."

skirts of the Clockwork Courtesan. "Jasmine and elderblossom," he noted, sniffing deeply. "Not scents applied to the garment of the Automaton but rather the unguents of the woman who came here and killed Sir Harry."

"Surely not, sir," Baxter blurted, unable to restrain himself. "She could not have left the room once the household was about, and we searched all the cupboards and other places of concealment when the body was found."

"Not all, Baxter. I said we were looking for a small man or a woman. Someone small enough to hide beneath the skirts of the Clockwork Courtesan here until you and Blakeney had departed, you to summon Mr. Eddington, Blakeney to calm the gardener's boy. That is how Frau Richtenhaus departed unseen."

"She was a-hiding in there when we found his body?" gasped Baxter, appalled.

Holmes assented. "It is clear that she serves a foreign power as a senior operative. She has been well trained. She entered Sir Harry Wickham's home by night, overcoming his locks, placing the drug in his personal tea caddy, then concealing herself in his museum."

I took up the account. "She took what she came for, silenced Sir Harry, then slipped off straight to the nearest post-master to send a message with the information Sir Harry had decoded from the movements of the mechanical bird at the Courtesan's shoulder; information contained in the ridges of the metal cylinder that determined the tune the mechanism plays!"

The man of business blinked in surprise. "Information?"

"Secrets smuggled into Britain for Sir Harry's Foreign Office employers," Holmes explained, his voice still muffled under the crinolines. "Secrets important enough to kill for, important enough for a foreign power to send an agent to sneak into our country and commit murder."

"I don't understand."

"A woman travelling under the name of Richtenhaus disembarked from a tramp steamer in London even as the Automaton arrived in Dover," supplied Holmes. "She left little trace and eventually lost herself in the teeming stews of Whitechapel. Her plans were disrupted by the unexpected theft of the Courtesan, but there Watson and I assisted her by accomplishing its timely recovery. She surfaced again to make enquiries of the horologist Melish and was clever enough to deduce the mechanism by which this mechanical lady—or her pet—might carry coded information."

I took up the explanation. "Lacking the key to the code she had to wait until Sir Harry had accomplished the translation. Then she stole both the notebook wherein he had written out the message and the original cylinder that had carried it. Sir Harry, the only other person this side of the Channel who knew the contents, was eliminated with a barbaric ruthlessness. Deuced unwomanly!"

"And you can catch this Frau Richtenhaus?" Eddington asked dazedly. "You can retrieve Sir Harry's notes?"

"There we are fortunate," Holmes declared. "Although she may have escaped back to the Continent, neither she nor Sir Harry realised that the information she had was incomplete." He opened the enamelled cabinet behind the Automaton and displayed the other nine iron cylinders in their storage case. "Each of these contains information. She has stolen one-tenth of the prize, Eddington. The rest is ours!"

I checked my watch. "It is almost five, Holmes," I warned. "We have a dinner engagement back in town. Perhaps we could take the cylinders for safe-keeping and examine them at Baker Street?"

"It would be easier to play them in situ here using the Courtesan's apparatus," replied the great detective. "Nor need we actually listen to the music. It is the bird's motions that require noting. Had Frau Richtenhaus realised that she might have silenced the music merely by not replacing the Courtesan's fan she would have avoided the attention of the gardener's boy that revealed the murder."

"If this woman has fled the country then the Courtesan will be safe enough for tonight," judged Lestrade. "We'll lock up this room and seal it tight and deal with the matter tomorrow when there's proper time for it."

And so we set the Clockwork Courtesan as a trap.

X

Holmes, Lestrade and I sat in absolute darkness and silence in Sir Harry Wickham's museum study. The only sound was the ticking of many clocks.

It was almost two when we heard the lock turning and the door was opened with furtive stealth. A narrow beam from a hooded lantern played across the floor.

We each slid loose our revolvers.

A dark figure padded across the floor towards the Courtesan.

Lestrade moved first, without waiting for Holmes' signal. "Halt there!" he called, throwing back the cover of his own dark lantern. "You are under arrest!"

The yellow light washed over the stricken form of Eddington as the man of business reached out towards the storage box beneath the Vienna Automaton. "Wait," the traitor gasped. "I can explain."

"Explain what?" I asked him coldly. "How you and Sir Harry were selling British secrets to some alien power? How you sneaked in tonight hoping for one final haul, the message borne by the Clockwork Courtesan? You disgust me, sir!"

"A trap!" Eddington realised. "You told me of the cylinders knowing that I would incriminate myself." He dropped his head into his hands. "What have I done?"

"You have betrayed your honour and your country," Holmes told him. "And you will stand for it before a jury of your peers."

"Jerome Eddington, I am arresting you on the charge of espionage," Lestrade said in the ponderous tones of an implacable guardian of the law. "Anything you say...."

He was cut short by the ratcheting of another pistol close by.

"Do not move," said the sleek young woman in black as she slipped in through the door that Eddington had left unlocked. "You are all armed but I have my gun already upon you. Place your weapons on the floor."

She had the advantage of us. Each of us, even Holmes, had been intent on the capture of Eddington. We had not been ready for Frau Richtenhaus.

Lestrade cursed as he tossed down his service revolver. I laid my own piece aside with more care. Holmes set his Browning at his feet. Frau Richtenhaus had us all step back from our discarded firearms.

"You'll never leave England alive!" Lestrade promised the dark beauty who levelled her pistol at us all.

"I have a poor opinion of policemen," she said, "although I admit to a mild admiration for the great Sherlock Holmes."

"The opinion is not mutual, madam," replied my friend. For him there is but one Woman, and Frau Richtenhaus was not she.

The spy tossed a satchel over to Eddington. "Fill this with the metal cylinders. Hurry." She kept the gun on us. "I had hoped to be able to record the cypher here but returning with the cylinders will have to suffice."

"So you were alerted by someone in the household to our earlier conversation!" I declared. "We hoped such loose talk would flush you out."

Her beautiful face darkened. "What do you mean?"

Holmes answered her. "It was clear that you had inside information regarding Sir Harry's domestic arrangements, madam. You knew his daily routine, down to his personal blend of tea and which caddy it was kept in. You had clearly suborned that information from someone in the

"You'll never leave England alive!" Lestrade promised the dark beauty.

household—Baxter or Milly, I would surmise."

"The maid," Frau Richtenhaus supplied, coldly betraying the domestic servant she had bribed. "The little fool sent word to me of what you revealed this afternoon."

"Then she drew you into a trap!" Lestrade warned. "Take them cylinder things if you please. There's no more secrets there. That was all a put-up talk, to drag Eddington and you back here where we could get you red-handed!"

Frau Richtenhaus snatched the satchel from Eddington and slung it on her shoulder. "That is not so," she denied; but of course that was exactly the trap that Holmes had laid to lure Sir Harry's killer back for capture.

Sir Harry's man of business sank to his knees. "What will become of me?" he moaned.

The foreign spy had no sympathy for a rival. "You will die with the rest," she told him. "I am not a fool. I will take these cylinders home and allow our finest minds to inspect them for whatever secrets they hold. Even if they hold none then I will still have accomplished my mission and returned in triumph!" She oriented her gun at Sherlock Holmes' head.

"Madame, I regret that I cannot allow your departure," he said.

"I can not see how you can prevent it," Frau Richtenhaus noted. Her English was as good as mine and her hand did not move as it presented the revolver. "Nor indeed can I see why I should not rid the world of a clever nuisance."

"Because this clever nuisance can tell you things which you need to hear," replied Holmes. "You have been used, Frau Richtenhaus. You have been fooled."

"Your trap? It has hardly had the result you hoped."

"Not that. Your mission was compromised before you had hardly stepped from your tramp-steamer onto the East End dock."

The woman's hand never wavered but her eyes narrowed. "Speak," she commanded. "My patience is small. Tell me what I do not know."

"You will pardon me if I place your actions in context for my friend and my colleague," Holmes replied. "Dr. Watson and Inspector Lestrade have not yet apprehended what you believed you were doing in Sir Harry's home."

"Speak!" Frau Richtenhaus demanded.

"By whatever undercover means this lady's employers used, Watson, they learned that some information of the most important kind was being sent back to England. Names. Names of men who were, I presume, sympathetic to British interests in the Baltic, men who had been found amenable to passing information or influencing policy that could resolve the crisis now growing in the region."

"Spies and traitors!" spat Frau Richtenhaus. "And dead now!"

Holmes shook his head, ruefully. "Not so, madam. You acted on the information you possessed: you apprehended that an additional cylinder had been added to Sir Harry's latest purchase, perhaps by the auction agent, van Groot, who had previously concealed messages in the clocks he acquired for Sir Harry at the government's expense. But this new data was so important that only the most Byzantine of transportation methods was deemed safe."

"The movements of the bird on the perch," I concluded.

"Exactly! I much admire the ingenuity of the man van Groot who must have recognised the unique use to which the Vienna Automaton might be put. Those motions of the bird on its ratcheted perch might easily translate into an alphanumeric iteration of the Playfair code that Sir Harry could interpret in the comfort of his own museum study. Frau Richtenhaus was sent to intercept those names and to deny them to both the British government and other nations that might suborn and usurp such agents."

The spy's head jerked back. "You already know that Wickham was selling his secrets?"

"I had inferred as much, given the state of his finances. The state might subsidise his horological collection for the sake of getting messages home but his accounts were still too healthy for a middle tier civil servant. Eddington here was his accomplice in peddling his secrets. That was why the man of business thoroughly searched Sir Harry's desk and removed what he could. He hoped for the translation Sir Harry had made of the Courtesan's message. He was thwarted."

"Because the cylinder and the notes had already been removed by this woman!" Eddington mourned. "Oh, God!" Her gun moved towards him momentarily.

"The Frau had to wait until Sir Harry had translated the message from the new cylinder," recounted Holmes. "That was why she concealed herself beneath the Courtesan until his work was done. Once the translation was complete and the drugged tea took its effect, she could emerge and verify the work."

"She checked the notation! That was why the gardener's lad heard music even after Sir Harry had bled to death." I looked over at the beautiful tiny woman. "But why cut Sir Harry's throat with the Courtesan's fan?"

Frau Richtenhaus smiled viciously. "Why not?" she demanded. "It amused me. His toy was his death."

Another thought occurred to me. "Those obituaries! Holmes, she has already sent the names of our allies and agents to her masters. Those deaths…."

"And more to follow," Holmes added. "But not of British agents."

Frau Richtenhaus' eyebrows lowered. "What do you mean?"

Holmes' glare was penetrating. "You blundered into an affair that was not meant for you, madam. You knew that Sir Harry was passing secrets to another foreign power? So, I'll warrant, did our British government. That is why they ensured that the names Sir Harry received on the cylinder were not the names of our agents."

The spy took a step forward. "Not your men? Of course they were! We know that van Groot sent the genuine information before he managed to melt away!"

Holmes accepted that. "Here I become tangled in this sordid mess. Yes, van Groot sent the names that the government needed. He added an additional cylinder, overlooking a slight dating problem that questioned the article's provenance. But you will recall that the Clockwork Courtesan did not go straight to Sir Harry from the docks at Dover."

"The theft!" exclaimed Lestrade.

"Indeed. A convenient theft, wherein the stolen merchandise was inspected en route for London. A theft which was so well conducted as to leave no trace save for a discarded glove with an identifiable pawnbroker's thread in it! Such an amateur mistake on so professional an operation allowed me to trail and retrieve the Automaton quickly enough not to disrupt Sir Harry's schedule of decoding and selling on the names on the cylinder."

"You mentioned that no arrangements had been made to pick up the Courtesan from the criminals," I recalled.

"It was always meant to be recovered, Watson. I was helped along to retrieve it in a timely fashion." Holmes looked over at Frau Richtenhaus. "That was so that a substitute cylinder with different names would fall into Sir Harry's possession and those false names would be sold on as genuine to his foreign buyers."

Frau Richtenhaus looked stricken. "You are lying," she said, but her voice betrayed her uncertainty.

"The man inspecting the stolen goods doubtless made the substitution. The names you stole when you murdered Sir Harry are the names that were supposed to be sent to whatever nation had suborned him—names of men who had no affiliation to the British cause but upon whom it served Britain to cast suspicion."

"No!" objected Frau Richtenhaus.

"Yes, madam. The men you named to your masters, the men they have eliminated, were loyal to your state but enemies of ours. As I told you, Frau Richtenhaus, you have been used in this matter no less than I."

The deadly woman had gone pale as she realised the magnitude of her error. "What have you made me do?" she demanded.

"For my part, nothing," my friend replied. "But I suspect that you have taken the bait laid out for a smaller fish and ensured the success of a dirty scheme far more effectively than ever Sir Harry and his man or business could have done." Holmes sniffed. "You have been a mildly interesting opponent, Frau Richtenhaus, but careless in verifying your facts. And now your career is at an end."

The spy cocked her weapon. "You forget who has the gun, Mr. Sherlock Holmes. I think my nation might be well served by denying yours access to your clever brain. I think your death might begin to pay for the destruction your government has wreaked upon loyal servants of B_____!"

I was about to hurl myself in front of Holmes and take the shot that would inevitably follow the lethal lady's speech, but Holmes said, "Hold, Watson. There is no need for heroics today."

At that moment Frau Richtenhaus clutched her neck as if stung by a bee. Her gun dropped from suddenly nerveless fingers. Her face assumed a rictus of horror as she stumbled to the floor.

"What?" I puzzled. How had my friend accomplished her downfall without even moving an inch?

Then three men in grey suits glided out of the darkness. Eddington yelped. I was reminded at once of the descriptions of the undistinguished persons that had commissioned and checked upon the work of O'Dwyer's gang. One of them knelt beside the fallen spy and plucked a tiny thorn from her neck.

"A derivant of curare," Holmes supposed. "In non-lethal doses Strychnos toxifera is a potent muscle relaxant."

"Who are these?" demanded Lestrade, reaching for his discarded firearm.

One of the men showed a paper to the Inspector. He blanched and stepped back, pocketing his weapon. His pinched face was more sour than ever.

"They work for the Crown?" I asked Holmes. "But...."

"They serve the state," conceded Holmes, frowning. "That is why these men have been following us ever since we began our investigation. That is why I allowed Frau Richtenhaus her moment of triumph. Villains who believe they have the upper hand are villains prone to talk."

"You knew these men were outside, waiting with a trap of their own!" accused Lestrade.

"They are undoubtedly skilled at their trade," my friend admitted. "I am a master of mine."

"Holmes!" I objected as the three silent men bundled up Frau Richtenhaus and made to depart with her.

"She is a valuable captive with much useful information," my friend told me, turning aside. "I doubt that Lestrade will ever be given the opportunity to bring her to trial."

"I expect not," growled the Scotland Yard man. "Gregson gets the credit for the Automaton's recovery and I get nothing, as usual!"[16] He watched mournfully as Eddington was marched off with the sleeping lady.

It seemed unjust to me too. "But she killed Sir Harry, Holmes! Even if the man was a traitor, selling our secrets to some enemy...."

"I doubt Frau Richtenhaus' future will be pleasant," Holmes replied. "Whatever happens to her and Eddington now are matters for the state. Our government, like all governments, keeps its dirty secrets. But come. Let us ask the man who arranged it for them!"

The Clockwork Courtesan looked on with shining glass eyes as the beautiful spy vanished forever. Like the perfect court lady she was, the Vienna Automaton would say nothing.

⚬

Mycroft Holmes betrayed nothing. His demeanour was as relaxed and lethargic as ever. He sat in his customary chair by his customary window in his gentleman's club, sipping his customary drink.

"The pawnbroker's glove was too gross," Sherlock Holmes to him. "Your planning was flawless, but you lack the practical experience to apply the fine detail."

"It served," the civil servant said. "You performed your role effectively. However, I am sorry to involve you and the good doctor in the unfortunate aftermath."

---

16 The rivalry of Inspectors Lestrade and Gregson was established as early as *A Study in Scarlet.*

"You planned to feed false information through Sir Harry," I recognised. "You couldn't know that Frau Richtenhaus would intercept it by murder and send it to those who would destroy the men named on the false cylinder."

"Could he not?" breathed Sherlock, contemplating his brother.

"There was to be war in the Balkans," Mycroft replied. "Now there is not."

There was an uneasy pause.

"You will extend our regards to our older brother when next you correspond with him?" Mycroft said at last.

"Of course," said Holmes. And we departed.

The End

On the Problem
of the
Detective Inspector That Didnt
Bark in the Night

One of the many considerations that a modern author attempting to produce a Sherlock Holmes story must face is how deeply to utilise Conan Doyle's wider supporting cast. On the one hand, the rich world of colourful characters that Holmes occupies is a chief attraction for lovers of the Canon. On the other, pandering cameos to elicit fan reaction or too much repetition of old tropes can push new works into amateur pastiche.

The difficulty is that Conan Doyle himself used his cast sparingly. Even Watson, who narrates almost all the Holmes stories and might be expected to reveal something of his own life, is niggardly with personal information. Apart from some passing comments on his military service, including brief allusions to a wound that migrates from shoulder to leg, and some accounts of Holmes' deductions about him based upon his pocketwatch, we are given remarkably little to go on. Holmesians have struggled to piece together even enough information to deduce that Watson married twice, possibly three times.

Beyond Watson the cast's backgrounds become even murkier. We see something of the rivalry between Inspectors Lestrade and Gregson and we hear of Holmes' good opinion of the latter; "the best of Scotland Yard" might be damning Gregson with faint praise, of course. We learn nothing of their rivalry's origin, and the theme is not revisited beyond *A Study in Scarlet*. Apart from broad physical descriptions of the various police officers who have suffered Sherlock Holmes in their investigations, we remain largely uninformed of their personalities and motivations. Lestrade and Gregson seem familiar to us compared to Inspectors Bradstreet, Hopkins, and the "tenacious as a lobster" Athelney Jones.

The same is true of Mrs. Hudson, Holmes' long-suffering landlady, the page Billy, the Irregular Wiggins, the gossipmonger Langdale Pike, and informer ruffian Shinwell Johnson. Readers would gladly know more of those cases requiring the shady muscle of the intimidating Shinwell or of how and when Holmes recruited his "street-urchin" investigative cohort; Conan Doyle elects not to satisfy our curiosity.

Thus fans are left to speculate. Mrs. Hudson was presumably the elderly widowed lady she is depicted as in films and images, but there is so little description of her in the stories that she could just as easily have been a attractive young war widow. Her first name may be Martha—"His Last Bow" mentions a female servant of that name—but apart from "her queenly tread" and Holmes noting in "The Naval Treaty" that "Her cuisine is a little limited, but she has as good an idea of breakfast as a Scotchwoman," we have no information on her at all. Debate even rages over whether that comment certifies her as Scots or rules out any Hibernian link.

New Holmes writers are inevitably tempted to fill in the gaps which Conan Doyle left. It would be satisfying to pen a story in which Wiggins or Mary Watson or Birdy Edwards the Pinkerton's Agent played a central role, wherein we could finally learn more about these fascinating Holmesian characters that we have so far only glimpsed.

The problem is that every time a new writer fleshes out background that Conan Doyle chose to leave unformed, that new story moves a little further away from the heart of the Holmes matter. No consensus exists to admit new facts to the Canon. A tale which establishes the further exploits of Miss Violet Hunter, in whom Holmes took an interest in "The Adventure of the Copper Beeches," would have no impact beyond the volume in which it appeared. The many literary returns of the fascinating Irene Adler have failed to stick and have often marked the fiction as "not quite proper" Holmesian material. We new writers can borrow the Holmes fan's indulgence for a while but we must understand the limits within which we can play with the toys in Conan Doyle's toybox.

All of this was very much in my mind when I wrote "The Adventure of the Clockwork Courtesan." This is now the fifth story I've produced for Airship 27's *Consulting Detective* series and I wanted to try the other kind of Holmes tale that Conan Doyle occasionally produced, the adventure yarn where Holmes rushed across his city and beyond, solving a case that was not a classic whodunnit with a limited range of suspects in a confined setting but rather interacting with his larger world.

That of course required consideration of which elements of that wider Holmesian creation to use to get the right "feel" without becoming too derivative. The rule of thumb I set was that if a character I would otherwise have to create already existed and had a good reason for appearing then I would allow the existing—and superior—character to appear.

Hence when the plot required a pair of Scotland Yard detectives it seemed appropriate to second Gregson and Lestrade and revive their mild professional rivalry. But I resisted sending Watson for expert assistance again from his friend Lomax at the London Library, as he had done in "The Illustrious Client," or having Holmes refer Sir Harry's business dealings to Mercer (from "The Creeping Man"), the "general utility man who looks up routine business"; such would have been crossing the line.

Then my plot required a clever and cunning government schemer, a master-planner who could baffle even Holmes for a time, the invisible puppet-master behind the tangle which killed Sir Harry and a half-dozen unnamed European enemies of the state but ended a war. It is difficult to introduce yet another non-Canon adversary with the cunning of a Moriarty or a John Clay[1], but fortunately Conan Doyle had already supplied another cast member with both the political position and intellectual acuity to provide the Great Detective with a challenge.

And I must confess that I was interested to work out what might happen should Sherlock and Mycroft Holmes' agendas not quite mesh, and I presumed that readers might be too. I hope that I have not done too much violence to the Conan Doyle-established relationships and situation outlined in "The Greek Interpreter," "The Final Problem," "The Empty House" and "The Bruce-Partington Plans."

All of which leads me to conclude that Conan Doyle knew his stuff; sometimes less is more. Sometimes it is the gaps which spark our imagination, not the framework around them. Sometimes the mystery is the magic, not its solution.

IW
Yorkshire, England, August 2011

---

1 "The seventh-smartest man in London" according to Holmes in "The Red-Headed League."

I.A. WATSON has contributed stories to the three previous *Sherlock Holmes: Consulting Detective* anthologies, of which his Volume 2 tale "The Last Deposit" won Best Short Story in the 2010 Pulp Factory awards. A sequel to his novel *Robin Hood: King of Sherwood* is now available. Look for *Robin Hood: Arrow of Justice* from Airship 27. The third and final Robin Hood novel is scheduled for release later in 2013. His work also features in he anthologies *Gideon Cain: Demon Hunter, Blackthorn: Thunder on Mars, The New Adventures of Richard Knight Volume 1, Blood Price of the Missionary's Gold: The New Adventures of Armless O'Neil Volume 1, Sinbad: The New Voyages, Monster Earth,* and *Alternate Visions,* and the novel *Blackthorn: Dynasty of Mars.* Details, additional free stories, and a scary author photograph are available at http://www.chillwater.org.uk/writing/iawatsonhome.htm

Sherlock Holmes

in

"The Problem of the Coincidental Glance"

By
Aaron Smith

*I*t was a rather boring day for us, one of Holmes' cases having just been resolved, the pieces put away neatly and the culprit behind a strange series of events in the custody of Scotland Yard. It was now the period of calm that typically came after the conclusion of the storm. I relished the rest, though Sherlock Holmes despised it. I took the opportunity to compose my notes on the case while the memories and details were still fresh and clear in my mind; my report of this case, like many others, would eventually be published. Holmes, on the other hand, if he had his way, would have preferred to be launched from one investigation into the next. It was only when he was on the trail of some malefactor or in the process of solving some seemingly impenetrable riddle that he was truly happy, like a predator in its natural environment. I sat with paper before me, pen in hand, about to begin jotting down what would probably have to be at least a dozen pages of notes, while Holmes stared out the window, looking down on the portion of Baker Street that lay below.

Suddenly, with no sign of warning, the calm of the morning was shattered by a loud cry from Holmes, followed by his throwing himself into a blur of swift motion.

"Aha!" he cried out, startling me. He spun away from the window, made his way across the room in the minimum possible number of long-legged strides, violently jerked his hat and coat from the stand where they hung, and bolted out the door like a man pursued by the hounds of hell! He said not a single word to me, no explanation of any sort. I could hear his footsteps pounding rapidly down the stairs, the front door being wrenched open and then slamming behind him.

I stood and went to the window. Down below, on the street, I could see Holmes walking quickly, purposefully, dogged determination in his every step, as if on some newly begun mission.

I had no way of knowing what had just happened. I could only assume that Holmes had seen something as he gazed out the window; something that had greatly alarmed him. I had no way of knowing where he was going, but I knew that had he wanted me to join him, he would have said as much. I sat back down, returned to the composition of my case notes, and waited for his eventual return.

X

Almost precisely one hour later I still sat at my work, scribbling down the details of the case I had set out to relate on paper. My task was interrupted by a bellowing voice coming from street level, cutting through the street sounds and clearly entering the window.

"Watson! Watson!" called the voice; it was unmistakably the voice of Sherlock Holmes, sounding alarmed and urgent. I went back to the window, opening it enough to stick my head outside. Looking down, I saw Holmes waving frantically to me. "Get your hat and coat, Watson, and come outside at once!"

I did as Holmes asked and flew down the stairs, past a startled Mrs. Hudson, and met Holmes just outside the door. He was breathless and red in the face when I found him, as if he had been running, exerting himself to reach our door as quickly as possible.

"Watson, listen to me!" he shouted, barely able to contain his excitement, trying not at all to conceal the tremendous urgency in his words. "The address is 136 Wickham! Go and find Lestrade or Gregson as quickly as you can! You must learn if there have been any sudden disappearances reported today or late last night. More specifically, any disappearance involving a young woman! If the answer is 'yes,' you must bring an inspector and several constables to that address as quickly as you can. The address, again, is 136 Wickham! Make no delay, Watson; a life may very well be at stake! I shall watch the place until you return. When you come, be sure that you and the police are armed!"

With that, Holmes turned and ran from the spot, back down Baker Street. Wickham Street, I knew, was ten blocks from our residence. Why Holmes should think that anyone might be in danger at that address I did not yet know, but I knew enough, from our years of working together, to trust his word and instincts enough to make haste in my efforts to reach the police. I hailed a hansom cab and ordered the driver to take me to Scotland Yard with all possible haste.

I reached Scotland Yard and gained entry with no delay, as a good portion of the men there were familiar with me, due to my association with Holmes. I found Inspector Lestrade, our frequent ally, in his office.

"Good morning, Watson," Lestrade said as he glanced up from the papers upon his desk. "What business brings you to my door on this fine day?"

"I apologize, Lestrade," said I, "but there is no time for formal greetings! I must know if you have received any reports of missing persons within the past few hours, specifically reports of young women having gone missing?"

Lestrade must have read the intensity of my expression and come to the logical conclusion that Sherlock Holmes had sent me and that it was a matter of importance, for he immediately called out into the corridor that ran past his office door.

"Roland, come in here!" he called out, and a uniformed sergeant came trudging in, a heavyset man with the belly of one who spent most of his working hours on desk duty.

"Yes, sir?" said the round sergeant.

"Sergeant, have we had any reports of anyone disappearing today? Or anything of that sort at all?" Lestrade asked, but Sergeant Roland shook his head.

"Sorry, Watson," said Lestrade, shrugging his shoulders. "What was it you expected to find here?"

I sat down and told him exactly what had happened that morning. I told him of Holmes running off after appearing to see something from the window, of Holmes' return and his subsequent instructions that I come to Scotland Yard and inquire about new reports of missing persons and, if such reports existed, bring Lestrade or one of his colleagues and a force of men to the specified address on Wickham Street. Lestrade nodded repeatedly as I told my tale. When I was finished, he scratched his head.

"Watson," he began, "I can't go runnin' off to Wickham Street with nothin' more than a hunch from Holmes! If the man had any real evidence that some bad business was happening at that address, he'd have busted the door down himself, I know him well enough by now and so do you! Listen, Watson, I'll lend you a constable, but that's the best I can do right now."

I could understand Lestrade's point of view quite well. Although I was sure that Holmes had good reason to be alarmed about the activity at that address, I still didn't know exactly what had aroused his suspicions. Lestrade could not very well be expected to leave his other work and rush off after Holmes' guess. I would have to settle for the single constable he was offering.

Minutes later, the man Lestrade had summoned walked into his office. I took one look at him and shook my head at Lestrade and walked right out of Scotland Yard alone. Constable Jones couldn't have even been twenty yet! I don't think he'd ever shaved in his life, so boyish did he look. It must have been among his first few days on the force! Lestrade had tried to lend me a child of a constable and I found this unacceptable. I'm sure the young man would grow up to be a fine policeman in time, but I couldn't very well drag a novice constable into a case of Sherlock Holmes', who certainly would not have the patience to deal with him. I left Lestrade and Jones where they stood and jumped into a cab outside the Yard, heading back to Wickham Street alone, hoping to find Holmes there to give me some explanation of what he had seen to set us off on this morning's activities.

)(

I soon found myself standing directly across the street from 136 Wickham Street. It was now late morning and the London streets were beginning to bustle with the usual heavy flow of pedestrians and carriages. I looked at the specified house across the way. It was as normal a building as one might expect to see, a simple two-story dwelling, probably containing a larger apartment below and, perhaps, two smaller sets of rooms above. There was nothing about it that gave me any cause for alarm. Of course, I have never possessed the eye for detail and detection that Holmes does.

Having found the address, I glanced around for some sign of Holmes. I saw many people nearby, but not him. I hoped he had not gone chasing after some suspect without me, for I hated the experience of having to wait for him to return, preferring to be a part of his game, no matter how small my assistance might prove to be. Then, from behind me, I heard a loud clearing of the throat, in a way that was meant to sound not quite sincere, as if a barely concealed gesture for getting one's attention. I knew what it was; it was Holmes, doubtless in some disguise by now, wanting to get my ear without crying out my name for all to hear.

I turned and found myself facing a dirty, disheveled creature of the streets, face smeared with grime, shirt too large, too loose and worn at the collar and elbows, trousers dirty, shoes ancient and ill-fitting, with a derby with a large hole in it perched atop his head. In his hand was a shoe shining kit.

I walked over to a bench that sat to the side of one of the street's shops. It would give me a place to sit down, while still allowing me to remain within visual distance of the mysterious 136 Wickham Street. I sat, produced a coin from my pocket, handing it to the shoe shiner.

Holmes knelt down in front of me and began to ply his temporarily adopted profession upon my shoes. I told him of my visit with Lestrade.

"Lestrade confirmed that there have been no reported disappearances, Holmes. With nothing but your suspicions, which I could not fully explain to him, as you have yet to explain it to me, he couldn't offer me more than a lone, very green constable, whose company I refused, suspecting his inexperience might hinder us unnecessarily. Now, Holmes, as I am of course willing to be of help to you in any way you require…would you kindly tell me what is going on here?"

"Of course, Watson," Holmes began, speaking just above a whisper, but clearly enough for his voice to cut through the sounds of people and horses trotting by. "As I looked out of our window today, I happened to see a certain man walking along Baker Street. Of all the morning pedestrians, my eyes happened to fall on this man and I instinctively began to analyze his appearance, as you have seen me do many times before with many other subjects of observation. There were certain details of his clothing and person which greatly alarmed me.

"He was about forty years of age, tall and of average weight for a man of his height. His posture and musculature suggested a manual laborer of some sort, perhaps a carpenter or other type of builder. Had I been able to have a closer look at his hands, I'd have been able to tell exactly what his occupation might have been. His clothing had surely not been worn while at his usual job, for I otherwise would have been able to tell his profession from his clothes.

"He was dressed quite normally for a man of the working class, in cheap but not necessarily poor quality pants, shirt, coat, and shoes. He wore no hat. Considering the early morning's rain, his lack of a hat was what first caused me to notice him, as nearly every other man who happened to pass down Baker Street had his head covered. His hat was missing and his hair was disheveled. This indicated that he had been hurrying for some reason, thus either losing or forgetting a hat. Something must have disturbed his hair as well, and in his hurry he neglected to put it back in place. As he passed, I could also see that his shirt was slightly opened at the place where it should have been closed by the middle button. It was open in such a way as to cause me to suspect, though I could not be certain from where I stood, that the button was no longer attached to his shirt in that spot. Also, he had a tear in his left coat sleeve, the sort of jagged tear that is usually made by a strong tug on the sleeve, strong enough to perhaps be the result of the strength that can be brought on during a desperate struggle, when the struggler is in a state of panic, perhaps fighting for dear life. Furthermore, I could see a distinct shoe print on his pants leg, a print of mud, staining his pants in such a way as to suggest that he had been kicked. It was in the shape of a style of shoe most often worn by young women.

"All this I observed when the front of his person was in view. As he passed below the window, I was able to see the back of his coat. There were, upon his back, several red streaks, what looked to me to be blood, traced there by the slim fingers of a woman being carried by this man!

"Putting all these observations together as I watched him pass, a picture formed in my mind. This man had struggled against a woman. He had injured her enough to spill some blood, although not very much. He had lifted her and carried her. She had been in a state of fear and desperation.

"All these facts led me to immediately suspect, at best, abduction. It may have been even worse, but I could see no signs of murder. Once my mind had confirmed what my eyes perceived, I shouted out and ran outside. I followed the man, from a safe distance of course, and trailed him to 136 Wickham Street.

"He went inside and still has not come back out. But look, Watson, look at the front steps leading up to the door. There upon the steps you can see the smears and smudges where the shoes of the young woman were dragged into that doorway. Our man must have dragged her there, and then left the house on some errand that brought him past Baker Street on his way back here! He must have taken her from some place, brought her here by carriage during the night—for otherwise someone would have seen her being dragged or carried along the street and summoned the police—and forced her up those steps and into that house!

"Once I was certain I had detected a crime in progress, I needed to alert you. Luckily, one of the Irregulars happened to be nearby. I had young Chester watch the place while I ran back to our rooms and sent you on your way to Scotland Yard. When I returned here, nothing had changed. I then sent Chester to fetch me his father's clothing and shoe shine kit so that I might conceal myself from anyone who might recognize me. Chester's father is in hospital with a flare-up of his old malaria, brought back from a long ago stay in a tropical prison, so he shall not miss his clothing for some time.

"That, Watson, is what brought me here to Wickham Street. In that house, a foul deed is taking place. I had hoped that some report of a disappearance had already been made, so that we might rely on the help of the Yard, but it appears that we shall have to rely only upon each other this time."

)X(

I was, as I had been many times before, stunned by the abilities and skills possessed by Sherlock Holmes. A chance look out of our window on a quiet morning had alerted Holmes to what appeared to be a dreadful event. Now we sat, perched on that street, wondering what to do next. Surely Holmes would have some sort of a plan in mind, so I continued to listen to him, not daring to interrupt.

"Blast it, Watson, I should have told you to bring down our revolvers when I called up to you at our rooms, but we shall have to do without them. Remain here; keep a careful watch on the front of the house. I shall leave this here," he said, depositing the shoe shine kit on the bench beside me, "and sneak around to the back of the house. Considering my present attire, should I be spotted I will be assumed to be a beggar and will most likely simply be chased away. Should I not be seen, I shall endeavor to look in any windows that I come upon. Come at any sounds of shouting or violence, but otherwise remain where you sit."

"Do be careful, Holmes," I implored him as he stood and made his way across the street.

Twenty minutes later, I still sat upon that bench, still waiting for Holmes to return. I had heard or seen nothing that gave me any cause for alarm, but was beginning to wonder whether I should approach the house myself, despite Holmes' orders. Just as I was growing more concerned about Holmes' failure to return, I watched as the front entrance door of the house at 136 Wickham flew open, to reveal the figure of the familiar shoe shine man standing in the threshold. Holmes waved a grimy hand, indicating that I should join him across the street. I stood and went to him. As I walked across Wickham Street, I noticed that Holmes had resumed his normal posture, straight and tall, which I took as an indication that the need for disguise no longer existed.

"Come inside, Watson, come inside," said Holmes as I reached the doorway where he stood.

I followed Holmes into the house and was surprised to see that the place was quite empty. Not a stick of furniture adorned the house's rooms. There was nothing. Judging by the accumulation of dust upon the floor and walls, it had been unoccupied for quite some time. There were some muddy footprints on the floor; being in Holmes' presence for so long had taught me the importance of looking for such marks.

"There's nothing here, Holmes," I said, stating the obvious.

"Yes, Watson, I had observed as much," Holmes replied, a droll humor in his voice. I knew from his tone that what I thought had occurred that morning was something very different from the truth, and I knew he was about to reveal that truth to me. He began to explain.

"When I made my way to the back of the house," Holmes said, "I heard the rear door of the house beginning to open, so I concealed myself behind the shrubbery and watched. Out of the back door came a man and a woman. Indeed it was the same man I had seen passing along Baker Street this morning! He had changed his attire and was now dressed in clean clothing which was not torn. With him was a lovely young lady, also clad in clean clothing. Both were laughing. The man held in his hands a cloth sack. As they passed by me, unaware of my presence, the man tossed the sack away, over the bushes. Luckily, the sack's contents were soft, for it bounced off of my head! They cut through the back yard of the lot and made their way out of my sight. As they passed, I noticed a plaster on the thumb of the woman's left hand.

"Once they were gone and I was alone, I opened the cloth sack and found the clothing the man had been wearing when I had first seen him. It was all there, the torn coat, the shirt with its missing button, the dirty trousers. Also in the sack were the disheveled and tattered clothing of a woman, including a pair of shoes that would match the shoes that made those marks I mentioned earlier, the marks on both the man's pants leg and on the front steps of this house."

I was quite surprised by what Holmes had told me. "Do you mean to tell me, Holmes, that the abduction of the young lady was faked?"

"Yes, Watson, that is precisely what I am telling you. Let us return to Baker Street. I will explain the rest on the way."

To my surprise, Holmes did not seem the least bit upset by what had just occurred. He had been tricked, drawn out in the pursuit of a mystery that was nothing but a well designed fraud! How could he not be angry, stunned, even outraged?

We walked back to our rooms, taking our time as the need for hurried pursuit was no more. Holmes began to speak again.

"Think, Watson, of the particulars of the matter which we concluded last night. Think of that case, for it connects directly with what has happened here today. What seemed to have finished last night was, in truth, only beginning. Now we near the end of that series of events."

I thought back to the previous few days. A British naval commander had been on his way to deliver some documents, papers detailing the location, somewhere off the coast of England, of a ship with a new type of engine, one which could increase the speed of naval vessels dramatically. He was to bring the papers to the residence of a certain admiral, a man who had certain health concerns that kept him from leaving his home, but whose mind was still the best there was at making important decisions regarding such nautical matters. The commander had been somehow lured off the most direct path and ambushed. He was left with a bad, but not deadly, head wound, and the papers had been stolen.

At that point, an appeal was made to Sherlock Holmes to find the thief and retrieve the papers. We were successful in our search for the man who had stolen the documents; the thief had been taken into custody by Scotland Yard. It was late when we concluded the chase and it was decided that we would keep the recovered papers at Baker Street until the following day, at which point Holmes and I would deliver them ourselves to the invalid admiral. When we had returned home that night, Holmes had handed the papers to me, still in their sealed envelope, and I had hidden them among some of my personal papers, thinking that should anyone attempt to steal them again they would search Holmes' property before sifting through mine.

As I finished thinking through my memories of that case, which I had thought concluded the night before; I realized why Holmes had brought the subject up.

"My word, Holmes," I nearly shouted, "They drew us out of our rooms so they could go in and search for those naval documents! We must get back there immediately!" I started to quicken my pace, but the hand of Sherlock Holmes upon my shoulder stopped me.

"No, Watson," he said. "Let them take what they have come for. As I said several moments ago, this matter has not reached its end."

※

By that point in our conversation, we had come within sight of 221 Baker Street. Holmes stopped in his tracks and I too paused. We looked across the street at our door. The door opened and, much to my amazement, out walked Sherlock Holmes! I knew, of course, that it could not be Holmes, for the real detective stood beside me, dressed in the shabby clothing of a shoe shine man, but the imposter was so well made up as to resemble Holmes in every respect! I gasped.

The imposter walking out the door of 221B Baker Street was made up as to resemble Holmes in every respect!

"Keep calm, Watson," said my companion. "Surely you did not think that I was the only man in London who excels at the art of disguise. As you know, there is the 'Napoleon of Crime,' Moriarty, who is equal to me in many skills, disguise being one of them. I have no doubt that he, with his own dexterous hands, applied the make-up to the face of that man, one of his many agents. As you know, Watson, the sabotage of our fine naval force is one of the professor's favorite hobbies. That man, a perfect doppelganger of me, surely has the papers you stashed among your belongings on his person now, as he exits our building."

"An agent of Moriarty," I said with shock. "We must stop him!"

"No, Watson, we must not," Holmes insisted. "This game must be played out in its entirety. I was much relieved that Mrs. Hudson left early today to go to market, for it would not have suited me to know that she was home when that imposter was present. Let us go inside, Watson, and try to make some order of the mess that man has surely left in his wake."

We made our way upstairs to our rooms, where we found the disarray that Holmes had predicted. Books and papers were strewn everywhere. I raced to my room, my hands falling upon the great heap of papers that had been tossed upon the carpeted floor. The envelope we had recovered from its thief was gone. Holmes came in behind me and put a reassuring hand upon my shoulder.

"Fear not, Watson," he calmly said, "for the real set of documents, containing the true location of that vessel and its prototype of the new sort of engine is safely hidden among the jars and bottles of Mrs. Hudson's pantry. The envelope I gave you to hide, the one that will soon feel the touch of Moriarty's guilty fingers, is a fake, and inside is a false location, where lies a ship that has no new engine, but only a dozen marines, waiting hungrily to get their hands on the coming saboteur."

I stood up, much relieved. "Holmes," I said, "you knew they would try to retrieve the documents once we had taken them into our custody!"

"Indeed, I did," Holmes explained. "I knew there would have to be some means of drawing us out this morning. When I saw the man pass by the window, I suspected that he was the bait, for he bore signs that I was sure to notice. I chose to take that bait, which I was reasonably, but not completely, certain was a ruse. To make my certainty complete, I sent you to see Lestrade. Had it been a real abduction, Scotland Yard might very well have had some report of it. That was Moriarty's one error in this game. Were I in his position, I would have falsified a report in order to complicate matters by bringing the police into the field of play. Other than that one small detail, our professor did exactly as I might have done had our positions been reversed."

"Incredible," I said in great admiration of what I had just learned.

Holmes turned towards the door of my room. "Put your papers back in order, Watson. Since Mrs. Hudson is absent, I shall go and brew us some tea. Then we shall sit and smoke for a while. In the later afternoon, we shall deliver the real papers to the admiral. I think we shall soon have word from the navy about an attempt to sabotage the decoy vessel."

Ж

Holmes' prediction proved accurate, as his predictions usually did. Two days later, we were paid a visit by a Captain Parker of the British Navy. We drank tea together as he told us of the three men who had been captured by the contingent of armed marines on board the ship that waited at the spot specified on the forged documents that had been taken from my room. The captain thanked us profusely and went on his way.

Shortly after he had left, Mrs. Hudson knocked upon the door. I opened it and she handed me an envelope, telling me that it had just been left by a messenger boy. I thanked her and looked at the sealed package. It was addressed simply to "My Dear Sherlock."

I handed the envelope to Holmes. He looked at it and let out a loud, hearty laugh. His long, agile fingers tore open the flap and he looked inside. He laughed once more and turned the envelope upside down. Like a winter's snowfall, a multitude of tiny flakes, shreds of document, fell to the floor in a cascade of torn white paper, upon which could still be seen small fragments of words and numbers.

"Watson," said Sherlock Holmes, "I am sorely tempted to try to reassemble these pieces, for I suspect that my counterpart may have placed some message, a warning perhaps, upon these sheets before tearing them thus. However, I find myself lacking the stamina for such a puzzle tonight. Perhaps in the morning, Watson; perhaps in the morning I shall try."

The End

An Ever-Present Friend

"The Problem of the Coincidental Glance" was one of three stories I wrote in preparation for the previous book (Volume 3) in this *Sherlock Holmes: Consulting Detective* series. I had such a rush of ideas for Holmes at the time that I came up with too much material. Having written three stories, I left it up to Editor Ron Fortier to choose the two that would be included. "The Adventure of the Mummy's Rib" and "The Adventure of the Injured Inspector" wound up in that book and this one was saved for Volume 4.

So, considering that this book's story was written several years ago, I'd be lying if I tried to talk about what was going through my head while writing it. The truth is that I simply don't remember. I suppose I was mostly just trying to come up with another good story. I hope I succeeded, but I'll let you be the judge of that.

What I would like to talk about then, is the strong presence that Sherlock Holmes, still my all-time favorite fictional character, continues to have in my life. I still sometimes can't believe I actually get to write Holmes stories that are published and read. I consider it an honor. But Holmes is, and always will be, far more than just the subject of some of my work. He's an icon, symbolic of what I feel makes a character great, and I see some of that in many, many different versions of Holmes, not just in the works of his true father, Sir Arthur Conan Doyle.

Doyle's stories influence my work a lot, not only my Holmes stories, but almost any time I'm writing a mystery of any kind. In fact, I'm currently working on a story in which the lead character, an editor of mystery novels, uses the mindset he got from a lifetime of reading Doyle and Christie and Rex Stout when he becomes an amateur detective to learn the truth about the death of his cousin.

I still occasionally pick up my thick old *Collected Sherlock Holmes* book and reread one of those old stories, and I continue to be a fan of many of the film adaptations of the character. My favorite, by far, is and probably always will be the Jeremy Brett TV adaptations. Brett was a perfect Holmes and Edward Hardwicke and David Burke were both excellent Watsons. Also among my favorites are the Basil Rathbone movies which, while sometimes straying far from the source material, are a hell of a lot of fun. I also enjoy the films featuring Arthur Wontner as Holmes, which are even older than the Rathbone version.

But there are many, many versions of Holmes on film, quite a few of them very good. In the time since the last volume in the *Sherlock Holmes: Consulting Detective* series of books, I've discovered two more versions of the Great Detective worth watching, both created for the small screen rather than the cinema.

When I first heard that the BBC would be doing a version of Holmes set in the modern era, I was skeptical. A big part of the appeal of Doyle's stories comes from its Victorian and post-Victorian setting and I wondered how the character could be made to fit in a world where the flow of information is faster and easier thanks to cell phones and the internet. I wasn't planning to watch "Sherlock", but I broke down and gave it a shot. I was very pleasantly surprised! They made it work. Benedict Cumberbatch (what a wonderful name!) is an excellent Sherlock Holmes. Martin Freeman makes a superb Watson. And the other characters, including Inspector Lestrade, Mrs. Hudson, Moriarty, Mycroft Holmes, and Irene Adler, were altered enough to fit into a modern setting while still retaining all the traits that made them fascinating characters when originally introduced to audiences well over a century ago. I'm currently enjoying the second season of "Sherlock" and looking forward to the eventual third season, which is set to begin production in 2013.

My other recent discovery is much older. In 1954, there was a British Holmes series that ran for 39 episodes and featured Ronald Howard as Holmes and Howard Marion-Crawford as Watson. Thanks to Netflix, I can watch that series whenever I want and it's quite good. It's a series of short little 20 minute mysteries with Howard almost perfect in the role of Holmes and Marion-Crawford playing a very good Watson, too. If Jeremy Brett is my favorite Holmes in straight adaptations of Doyle's stories, Ronald Howard is (so far) my favorite Holmes portrayer in stories written specifically for TV. I was delighted to discover the series.

So, as a Holmes fan, it seems there are always new versions of the Great Detective to discover. I can only hope that some other fans of the character might find my Holmes stories in this and other books and judge them to be worth reading. I can never compete with Sir Arthur Conan Doyle. The character belongs to him and always will, but I hope I can add something to the ever-growing number of Holmes stories out there for fans to enjoy once they've read those wonderful originals.

I hope to write more Holmes stories in the future. But whether I do or not, the greatest detective in fiction will be a character I'll cherish in many of his incarnations.

AARON SMITH is the author of 26 published stories, many of them for Airship 27 Productions. His pulp work includes stories in both volumes of *Black Bat Mystery*, four Sherlock Holmes stories, the Dr. Watson novel *Season of Madness*, and stories featuring Ki-Gor, Dan Fowler, and his own creations, Hound-Dog Harker and the Red Veil. His latest novel is *100,000 Midnights* from Musa Publishing. Information about his work can be found on his blog at www.godsandgalaxies.blogspot.com.

Sherlock Holmes

in

"The Adventure of the Black Katana"

By
Bradley H. Sinor

I have on occasion wondered how Mrs. Hudson would have reacted the day when my friend Sherlock Holmes and I came to live at 221B Baker Street, had she known the people and situations that would find their way to her door at all hours of the day and night. I would like to think she would have shrugged and asked what time we would like breakfast.

Of course, that morning in early June, 1894, when Mrs. Hudson appeared to announce the arrival, not of a client, but of an old friend of mine, I hardly expected things to be as unusual as they turned out.

"Dr. Tobias Black," she said. "To see Dr. Watson."

"Toby Black!" I said "Now that is a name I have not heard in years."

"A medical colleague?" said my old friend, Sherlock Holmes, who sat with his long legs stretched out in front of the fireplace.

"Indeed he is. We served together in Afghanistan" I said.

It had been into his hands that my orderly, Murray, had given me over, after carrying me out of the line of fire when I received the wound that had nearly killed me, that had eventually invalided me back to England.

"Then by all means bring him in, Mrs. Hudson!" said Holmes. "A reunion of old friends is always a good way to start the morning."

What amazed me was the fact that Toby had located me. I had only just completed my relocation to 221B Baker Street in the last week. Holmes' return, after what several of the news journals had christened 'The Great Hiatus,' had been well covered. I had, thankfully, not been a major part of the story.

Tall and as lean as Holmes, Tobias Algernon Black carried himself in a manner that took me back to the battlefield hospitals in Afghanistan.

"It has been far too long, old man," he said, taking my hand.

"Indeed it has, Toby," I said, directing him to a chair opposite mine. "What brings you into London? The last I knew you were still serving in the army, no doubt in the middle of every hot spot in the Empire."

"One does what one has to," he chuckled. "There has been more than one battlefield that I made it out by the skin of my teeth."

"Knowing you, even with a general's direct order, it would have taken a couple of burly sergeants on each of your arms to get you to leave," I said.

"Watson, I'm shocked, shocked, that you would think I might disobey direct orders from a general officer. I do admit that on one or two occasions when I made my exit, there might have been a pair of sergeants similar to what you mentioned in the area," he said casually. "Although I defy you to look me in the eye and say you wouldn't have been right beside me."

That was the Toby Black that I remembered; his patients came first even over his own safety. More than once that had brought him to the edge of disaster and given some tall tales to be told about him in the officer's mess.

"Yes, I would like to think I would have been right there beside you," I said.

"I know you would have been." Toby's face went serious. "Watson, I read of the passing of your wife. My deepest condolences."

"Thank you, it was her heart, a congenital family condition; her mother and several cousins suffered from it. We knew her health was tenuous; I just hoped we would have more time than we did."

A few months previous I would have not been able to speak even that much regarding Mary. The pain of her loss was still there, and would always be there, but the good memories had begun to override the painful ones. I also knew that she would be angry with me if I wallowed in the pain of her loss.

"Life is like war sometimes; you never know just how long you have. If the death and devastation of war can be said to teach us anything, it's that we need to appreciate those we love and what time we have together," said Toby.

I most heartily agreed.

"But you are retired from the army, now, in fact you've been staying in the north country for some time," said Holmes casually. "I'm glad to see that you were able to bestir yourself from that quiet countryside and come to London, which you don't seem to frequent that often."

I'm not sure which amused me more, Holmes' comment or the astonished look on my old army friend's face.

"Mr. Holmes, I have read all of Watson's accounts and know that you no doubt pieced together that information from a number of things you have seen about my person," said Toby. "I would like to think that I have a logical mind, so let me see if I can follow your line of reasoning."

"A man after my own heart," said Holmes with a smile. I had seen few others come anywhere near Holmes' prowess; there was that fellow, Barker, but he was a whole other story. "Watson knows my methods, and has on more than one occasion used them well. Let us see how well you do."

"Thank you, Holmes," I said, sadly recalling my attempt to deduce the details of a mystery visitor some years ago based on a walking stick that had been left in our quarters. Tobias Black looked down at his trousers, ran his hands over the sleeves of his jacket, then seemed to withdraw into deep thought for a few moments.

"I think I have some of it, Mr. Holmes," he said finally. "but definitely not all of it."

"Pray share your conclusions with Watson and myself," said Holmes.

"Very well," our visitor said. "My residence is indeed in the north, in Sandburough, not that many miles from the Scottish border. I suppose that you might be familiar with my family, but I doubt it, given the examples that Watson has published of how your mind works. Therefore I would say that piece of information was discerned from the train schedule in my overcoat pocket."

"Excellent, Dr. Black," said Holmes. "You are observing, as well as just seeing, something that far too few people actually do. Is there anything else you would care to mention?"

"I'm at a loss for the rest of your deductions. I am sure they are basic bits of information, but I am missing them."

I could see the curiosity in his eyes, the same expression I had seen in many others' who had sat in front of Holmes, not to mention, I suspected, in my own face when I awaited the explanation for my friend's deductions.

"You are correct that the train schedule gave me the probable location of your home. True, you could be traveling there on business, but I think not, since the particular train you have circled is an express and scheduled for the late afternoon. If you were traveling on business it is more likely that you would be on a morning or evening train. So therefore you are more than likely returning home.

"Now, as to your being retired from the army. You still have the bearing of a military officer, not to mention my notice that you are wearing a stick pin that bears the insignia of a military unit that was formed only in the last five years. Given that you are not in uniform and have been living for some time in the north, it is not too unreasonable a stretch to say that suggests a retired officer. I am correct, am I not?"

I was certain that Holmes was one hundred per cent accurate. He made mistakes in his deductions, but they were few and far between.

"Indeed you are. I retired two years ago, shortly after the death of my father, Alexis Black, to manage the family estates and business.

"I tell you, Watson, there have been more than one time since then that I would cheerfully have returned to India and Afghanistan; being in combat there would make more sense than facing the insane world of corporate board rooms. Thankfully, I don't have to come to London very often. I have a number of excellent managers," he said.

I looked over at Holmes. "And how did you know he did not come to London very often?"

"When Dr. Black put his gloves away, two tickets for last night's performance of the Gilbert and Sullivan operetta "Utopia, Limited" fell on the floor. While it did open last year, this could have been for a second viewing. But, given the reviews, I sincerely doubt it, so it seemed likely that it was an initial viewing and therefore he had not been in London any time in the near past."

I must confess that for a moment I wasn't sure if I was more surprised by his deductions or the fact that he paid any notice to the public reaction to Gilbert and Sullivan.

"I am amazed, Mr. Holmes" said Black. "Yes it was an initial viewing. Quite good."

"So what brings you up to London this time, Toby?" I asked. "While it is nice to see you, I hardly expect it was just to visit an old army companion?"

Tobias Black took a long deep breath, apparently having to steel himself to tell the reasons that had brought him to Baker Street.

"It is on the matter of a burglary of my family home, just over three weeks ago. I am hoping that Mr. Holmes can help me in this matter," he explained.

"The details, sir, all the details. You say the event took place three weeks ago. I should have been called in then. Now any evidence may have been wiped away with the passage of time," he said, slumping back in his chair.

"Three weeks ago, Holmes," I reminded him, "You were still 'dead,' so calling you in might have proved more than a bit difficult."

"Quite true," he admitted. "The facts, sir, let us start with what was stolen."

"For a number of years my father had numerous business interests in the orient, Japan specifically. During that time he acquired a rather extensive collection of items from the island: books, artwork and weapons. While I admired by father's enthusiasm for his hobby, I have no interest in it and decided, since he is no longer with us, to donate the collection to the British Museum. My father enjoyed them and my family has as well, but it's time that the public is given a chance to view part of that amazing culture."

"That is most commendable, Dr. Black. Would that more private collectors took that stance. So tell me, have there been any other burglaries in the area, before or since?" asked Holmes.

"None that I am aware of. I made a report to our local constable about the burglary, but they were not able to find any trace of the criminal or, for that matter, just how they got into the house. In fact, the display cases were still locked and there was no sign that anyone had opened them for days."

"I'm not surprised. The minions of Scotland Yard who are assigned to the rural districts are rarely, if ever, of the top level of skill," Holmes opined. "What was stolen?"

"Only a single item: a samurai's sword, called a katana. It is nearly two hundred years old. It is one of only a few blades surviving that were made by the sword master Hikaru Takei."

"Has there been any trace of the stolen item? I imagine the market for stolen Japanese material is somewhat limited: museums and a number of collectors."

"Are you saying that one of the museums might purchase stolen items?" I asked. Even as I spoke, I realized just how naïve that sounded.

"Unfortunately," agreed Toby. "And it is not just in other countries. There are any number of public and private museums that would turn a blind eye to such activities if it would result in their adding a major piece such as that blade to their collection. I have made inquires among several smaller museums with Japanese items in their collections as to whether they have been approached about the sword."

"Excellent, Dr. Black, I must compliment you on having a very devious mind," said Holmes. "What were the results of your inquiry?"

"I came up with absolutely nothing. I was at my wits' end. I considered going again to Scotland Yard. However, they are, of course, more concerned with current cases rather than a country home break-in that is now weeks old."

"Yes, an unfortunate situation with the law enforcement community. The passage of time dims their memories, although it does not erase them. On my first visit to Scotland Yard after my return to London, Inspector Lestrade mentioned that they had finally found the final bits of evidence that they needed to put down a case that has been lingering in their files since before my…extended holiday abroad."

"Would that have been the Mannering kidnapping?" I asked.

"Indeed it was. It turned out to be the adopted son's maternal aunt," said Holmes.

"Then I read in the papers of your return, Mr. Holmes. I am hoping that you are not already overwhelmed with matters and could give me your

"What was stolen?"

advice on this one."

Holmes stood up, stretching himself to his full height. He did not speak for several minutes but began to pace slowly across our sitting room, stopping at the chess board where the game that he and I had left off the previous evening stood awaiting our return.

"Doctor, you are correct. Since my return to London I have found myself with a plethora of cases. Watson has filled two notebooks with his records of just these," he elaborated.

"I was afraid of that, Mr. Holmes. I would not expect you to put aside any of them to deal with a minor country house burglary. Watson, I plan on being in London for another two days. Perhaps you can join me at my club for dinner and a few hands of whist," Toby said, rising and looking toward the place on the wall that his coat and hat were hanging.

"Toby, I would enjoy that very much, although I will warn you that my skills with cards have improved considerably, or at least I would like to think that they have done so."

"I look forward to it."

"Doctor. you are leaving?" said Holmes, as if he had only just become aware of Toby's movement toward the door

"Yes. I wish you had been able to take on my case, but I fully understand the matter of a large caseload."

Holmes took his pipe and stared at the bowel for a long moment. "As I mentioned, I do have a number of cases on the docket, however, your situation does have aspects that intrigue me. For an old friend of Dr. Watson's, I will be happy to look into the matter."

⋇

"Dr. Watson! Dr Watson!"

Being awakened, from a sound sleep, in the middle of the night is a fact of life for a doctor. So I was not at all startled to find Mrs. Hudson standing over me, a candle in her hand. From the tolling of a church steeple, in the distance, I knew that it was one o'clock in the morning.

"Yes, Mrs. Hudson," I said, shaking my head clear of the cobwebs.

"There's a gentleman downstairs to see you, a police officer."

"Did he say what this was about?"

"No, doctor, only that Mr. Holmes had sent him to fetch you."

I was up and dressed in less than five minutes. Holmes had left early in the afternoon saying that he had things to look into before he could consider dealing with the matter that Toby Black had laid before him.

The policeman was a tall, lean man in plain clothes; a scar cut across his right cheek from his ear to the edge of his mouth; his curly hair peeked out from a battered bowler and the lower half of his face was wrapped in a scarf. Mrs. Hudson had escorted him into our sitting room. The man stopped and stared at the fireplace mantel where a portrait of the Reichenbach Falls hung. I had told Holmes that the memories that the picture conjured up of his supposed death and, then, three years of wanderings were something that should be put away.

"It's a reminder, old friend, that I should never take any situation for granted. After all, with only a few subtle changes to the narrative, it would have been me laying at the bottom of those waters, not our old friend Moriarty," he chuckled.

I stopped at my writing desk and picked up my army revolver; it was loaded, and I dropped half a dozen additional shells into my pocket. I doubted that it would be needed, but my years at Holmes' side had taught me that it was far better to be safe than sorry in many situations.

"Sorry for the delay," I said to my visitor as I picked up my medical bag, glancing inside to make certain that I was not lacking anything. I then took my hat and topcoat from where they hung.

"Think nothing of it, Doctor. My name is Carradine. We do need to be on our way. Mr. Holmes told me to bring you along right away."

"Then let us be away," I told him. "Can you tell me what the situation is?"

"Mr. Holmes said I should wait and let him brief you. I have a cab waiting for us outside."

That sounded just like Holmes.

){(

It took nearly a half hour for us to make our way from Baker Street into the warehouse district near the Thames estuary. The buildings in this area had the look and feel of places that would have made the East End feel like a marked improvement for anyone who was forced to live in there.

During the entire trip my companion said virtually nothing beyond the occasional direction to the driver. I tried to elicit some sort of information regarding the case, but soon realized that it was a waste of time.

There was light coming from one of the buildings, where a number of uniformed officers and men that I took to be detectives were standing around the entrance. A cold breeze whisked up the street, bringing the smell of the river and a chill that enveloped the whole scene. I pulled my overcoat a little tighter and headed for the main warehouse door. I recognized several unformed officers lingering about.

My companion spoke with two of the plainclothes officers before coming around to my side. The man then turned and motioned to several other men who had been examining a crate with the words Miskatonic University painted on its side. One of them handed my escort a clipboard, pointing out several items on the pages.

The inside of the building was as run down looking as was the outside. Yet, amazingly enough, there were crates and items wrapped in protective blankets that filled the inside of the building almost to overflowing. A number of men seemed to be systematically searching the area.

"If you will follow me," he said finally, turning his attention back to me. "I believe Mr. Holmes is waiting for you in the manager's office, Doctor."

Since it was obvious I was going to get no more information from this man, I did as I was told and went into the office. A pair of candles sat on the rather worn-looking desk, so covered with papers that they were dropping off onto the floor.

"Ah, there you are, Watson," said Holmes. But the words came not from Sherlock Holmes, but rather his brother, Mycroft Holmes.

I confess I stood there rather slack-jawed for a few moments. Seeing Sherlock Holmes' older brother in any other environment than the confines of the Diogenes Club or 221B Baker Street was, to say the least, a shock.

"Good evening, Dr. Watson; won't you please come in. The evening is rather chill and this warehouse is definitely not heated. My apologies for not alerting you that the detective that collected you was my emissary rather than my brother's."

He directed me toward a chair near his own. There were several candles arranged on the desk to give the maximum amount of light. The office itself bore the chaos that was normal for such a place: boxes piled hither and yon; clipboards full of records hanging on the wall; several large filing cabinets, one of which was sitting open. The contents, at least I presumed that is what I saw, were spread out on the table.

It had been nearly a year since I had crossed paths with Mycroft Holmes. My friend, A.J. Raffles, had invited Mary and myself to a special charity presentation of the Gilbert and Sullivan operetta, "The Pirates of Penzance." Apparently it had been at Mycroft Holmes' direction. I had been summoned backstage to care for one of the actors who had become ill. I didn't learn until much later that there had been an assassination attempt that night against the Prince of Wales.

That had been one of the last evenings out that Mary and I had shared; she was taken from me not long after that.

I have elsewhere described Mycroft Holmes as being a heavyset man, which he actually is not. He is large but not nearly as corpulent as the ever-talented Mr. Sidney Paget portrayed him. It was actually an idea of his brother's to present Mycroft Holmes thusly, in order to confuse any possible enemies whom he had made because of his government duties.

"Obviously, you did not summon me here for tea or simple conversation. So what is it you need of me?" I asked.

The man that Sherlock Holmes had once described as 'occasionally being the British government' directed my attention to a sheaf of papers lying near the edge of the table.

"If you would be good enough to have a look at those documents and give me your thoughts on them, I would be most grateful."

I picked up the aforementioned papers and began to leaf through them. There were several dozen; most were covered in a precise-looking but crabbed handwriting, along with sketches and annotations to the latter. It was quickly obvious that these were medical records, basic medical histories, the sort of notes that any competent doctor would make concerning the patient in his care.

After reviewing the pages a second time, I set them down and looked over at the elder Holmes. He had been watching me without a word, obviously looking for some reaction concerning the contents of these records.

"And?" I said, putting the ball in his court. "What is so special about these medical histories that you could not consult with the doctors that the Diogenes Club has on call normally, and that you had to summon me in the middle of the night?" I asked.

"The Diogenes Club is a gentlemen's club, nothing more," huffed Mycroft Holmes. "But you are correct; there is something unique about these documents. Both of these men have been murdered in the last seventy-two hours."

Statistically this was nothing unusual, but given the source of this information, I knew that there was far more involved here than met the eye.

"I still haven't gotten one vital answer, though I freely admit to having far more questions than answers at this point," I said looking at Mycroft

Holmes. "You have yet to tell me just why you wanted me involved in this case. I still think you would have been better suited to have summoned your brother to look into this matter."

"What makes you think he didn't," said Carradine, who had been standing quietly to one side of the office this entire time. The man next to whom I had spent a half hour sitting as we traveled here from Baker Street stepped up beside Mycroft Holmes. He began systematically to remove the dark scarf and the curly hair wig, along with pulling the fake scar from his cheek; changing his appearance in just the way he stood.

"You did it again, Holmes," I admitted.

"A thousand apologies, Watson. From the moment that Mycroft briefed me on this matter, we both knew that neither of us seem to be overtly connected with him. Yet it was necessary that you learn the truth, so if you were seen being brought here by those who habitually watch my brother, then it would look like you were consulting with him on an entirely different one of Mycroft's little escapades."

Holmes stretched himself, expanding to his full six foot two inch frame.

"Really, Sherlock, I would appreciate it if you would approach this matter more seriously, as it is a matter of the national interest," said Mycroft Holmes.

Sherlock Holmes nodded to his brother. "As you know, I am all too well aware of the situation and know just how troublesome it might be. You must excuse us, Watson. Let us say that siblings do, at times, have differing opinions on matters."

My hand moved to my vest pocket where my older brother's watch sat as it had for the many years since his passing. I remembered the disagreements that my brother and I had, sometimes on the smallest of matters. It actually did my heart good to see that the Holmes brothers disagreed on things, even if I was not yet privy to the details.

"So, again, why me? From everything I have learned of you, Mr. Holmes, I know you have good reasons for what you do, even if it means not involving your usual resources." That brought a smile to Holmes' face; his older brother simply acknowledged my comment with the slightest nod.

"My brother describes you as one of the most trustworthy people he has ever known; my own resources verify that evaluation. I need someone that I can trust to look into a matter that may have international implications."

While it didn't hurt my ego to hear comments such as that, I did feel more than a twinge of uneasiness at Mycroft Holmes' words.

"There is another reason that I had Sherlock bring you here tonight.

While it is true that I did not want to involve the normal channels that I have at my disposal, the matter is of an extremely delicate and possibly scandalous nature."

"You know of my discretion." I said. There were several dozen cases involving Sherlock Holmes that I had chosen not to make public, some at Holmes' request, others because I felt that the world was not yet ready to know the true nature of them. There were still other matters that I had learned of during and after my residence at Baker Street that I had not even put on paper, matters that I felt should not be put to paper, now or perhaps ever.

Mycroft Holmes templed his fingers for a moment, the action reminiscent of his younger sibling. "Indeed I do, doctor. Let me explain that the two dead men had in the past acted at the behest of Her Majesty's government on a range of matters, mostly in the eastern portions of the empire. They were well versed in keeping certain events out of the tabloids next to headlines reporting New Forest murders. They had a third partner in their assignments: your old friend, Dr. Tobias Black.

"I strongly suspect that the recent theft at the Black manor house has something to do with this entire matter. However, it is vitally important that no connection ever be made between myself and Dr. Black. Hopefully, any observers—and trust me they are out there in the night—will think I have summoned you in regards to another matter," said the elder Holmes. "Now, as to the reason I asked you here, Dr. Watson, it is to examine the bodies of the murdered men. Cursory examinations have been made, but I feel an unbiased look at them by you might provide additional information."

"I am at your disposal, sir," I said.

Ж

There is a distinctive smell to morgues not found anywhere else in nature; part is the purification of flesh, mixed in with the disinfectant that the attendants are supposed to use in copious amounts. But there is something else, something more indefinable. If I were more of a philosopher I would say that it was the actual smell of death itself.

This was not the central morgue, located near the coroner's courtroom, but one in the basement of a small hospital.

"If you will come this way, sir," the morgue attendant said.

I had been supplied with documents that gave me authority to examine the bodies. The attendant examined the papers, nodded and said little else.

Given the hours that these men spend with the dead, I had observed they either became complete chatterboxes, seeming to relish the company of any of the living, or as silent as those who are in their care. This one was the latter, with which, given the hour and the circumstances, I had no problem.

He took me to a room at the end of the hall. The tables in the room were both occupied, I presumed, by the bodies I had come here to examine.

"I'll fetch you a set of instruments, doctor, along with a copy of the paperwork; I think the full autopsy isn't set until Friday. There are several aprons to protect your clothing in the cabinet. That's Mr. Goldman on the left and Mr. Malone on the right."

With that the man was gone. I heard his footsteps on the brick floor fading down the hallway.

I turned my attention back to the bodies. Since Goldman was the closest, I began with him.

He was in his mid thirties and looked as though he would have been able to defend himself against any normal street ruffian who might attack. I guessed the attack had been swift and sudden, no friend suddenly attacking, in this case.

What puzzled me were the wounds, themselves. The killing blows had not come from a knife or an ax or a butcher's blade. No, this damage had been done by something long and obscenely sharp. Whoever had wielded it seemed to know what he was doing.

"A sword?" I muttered to myself. Given the involvement of Toby Black in this matter, I wondered if his missing sword might have been the murder weapon.

The attendant reappeared with a tray of instruments and the paperwork he had mentioned.

"Excuse me," I asked him. "Do you recall if the policemen who brought these men in mentioned if there was a lot of blood at the scene?" I knew that people like to gossip about horrific crime scenes, and while it was possibly mentioned in the reports, it could be buried in bureaucratic morass.

"As a matter of fact they did. The officer said that Mr. Goldman was lying in a lake of his own blood. It were a messy sight, one of them wondered if maybe ole Jack boy had come back and weren't targeting women any more."

From the man's tone I knew that he didn't believe it, and the fact that he was apparently operating under orders from Mycroft Holmes was the only reason that I didn't caution him about spreading rumors. This wasn't the work of the Ripper; Druid's Hill Asylum's security had not been and would not be breached, so that was one fear that would not come true.

"Under the circumstances, I think we agree: the murder weapon was probably our missing katana. As always, your reports are thorough and exact, old friend," said Sherlock Holmes. "I just wish that you would bring some of that same exactness to your published records of my cases. Let the readers know the facts, which the romantic adventure that you inject into my work tends to obscure."

I had long ago lost count of the number of times Holmes had complained about my stories not being just plain recitation of the facts. Although I have always suspected that Holmes enjoyed reading my stories, though he would never admit it, several times I had seen him with a copy of The Strand magazine on the table next to his chair.

We arrived in Sandburough just after ten in the morning, which suited me quite well, since the trip had allowed me to catch up on some sleep as well as work on notes for another of Holmes' cases, which I called "The Matter of the Extinct Crane."

The train had been delayed twice, putting us some three hours behind the announced schedule, yet my companion had hardly moved. Were it not for the occasional shift in his eyes and the regular rising and falling of his chest, I would have wondered if he were still alive. Yet no sooner had the train pulled into the station, he came fully to life and moved quickly to hire a cart and have the porter fetch the small traveling cases that we had brought with us.

The country around Sandburough that led toward the Black family home was actually quite beautiful. As the cart made its way toward the house, we passed over two large and very active branches of a river that I suspected had its birthplace miles north of here in Scotland. I caught myself looking at the water and wondering just how ripe those waters might be for trout; it was a sport I had not indulged in for nearly two years, as Mary's health and my practice had prevented any extended fishing holidays.

"I would say that you would stand an excellent chance of reeling in several specimens of trout," observed Holmes as if having read my mind. "Don't look so astonished; knowing your fondness in the past for fishing, when I see you staring with interest at a river it is a better than average possibility that wading hip deep into the waters is not far from your thoughts. Plus, in my research on this area, I did come across the information that the waters here are rife with fish at this time of year."

"Clearly, Holmes, your powers are still as sharp as always."

Holmes waved the compliment off. As the cart pulled along the long drive up to the Black home, I stared at the place. It was one of any number of sturdy residences that could have been built any time in the last decade or the last century.

Surprisingly, Toby did not greet us at the door. His butler, a large, rather intimidating fellow with salt and pepper hair who identified himself as Creighton, welcomed us. He directed us to the study where Holmes and I found Toby sitting in a large overstuffed chair, his leg propped up on a footstool on top of pillows. Next to the chair was a pair of crutches.

"Toby, what the devil has happened?" My first thought was that the unknown assailant had had at him, with my old army comrade being far luckier than his two associates in Mycroft Holmes' service. Although, when I saw the embarrassed look on his face, I knew at once that it was nothing quite so dramatic.

"Let me have a look at that ankle of yours. Please don't try to give me any tall tales about how you have treated it yourself. You know how bad an idea it is for a doctor to have himself as a patient."

My wife had, on more than one occasion, pointed out that while I might be an excellent doctor, I was myself a miserable patient.

"Very well, I surrender myself to your care," he said. "Mr. Holmes, while John pursues his oath to Hippocrates would you be good enough to pour me a drink and one for yourself?"

"Indeed, I will," said Holmes. Out of the corner of my eye I saw him pour glasses of sherry for all three of us.

Truth be told, Toby had actually done a good job in bandaging his leg. After a little judicious probing I found that nothing appeared to be broken, just badly bruised. I suspected that he had rolled into the fall instead of trying to stop himself as he crashed to the floor. It might have been undignified and the end been painful, but it also kept the bones from breaking.

"So what happened?" I asked.

"Well, it's my own damned fault, really," he replied. "I arrived home late yesterday afternoon. Creighton was seeing to my bags. I had taken a couple steps up the stairway when the cook called my name. I turned and it seems that I was only partially on the step. That action sent me tumbling head over heels down to the landing."

I couldn't help but laugh. I knew it was not funny to my friend, but the mental image of him tumbling down like a marionette that had had its strings cut was quite amusing.

"I will point out," I reminded him, "that at least you didn't end up in the middle of the roses."

"Watson, you would remember that little incident. I had hoped that it was buried and forgotten," he grimaced.

Holmes cocked an eyebrow at me but said nothing. During our time in Afghanistan, Toby, as had a number of the other young officers in the Fifth Northumberland fusiliers, become besotted with the daughter of our company commandant. One evening he had attempted to climb the trellises leading to her room, intending to recite poetry to her. Unfortunately, that structure had proved too weak and he had ended up in the middle of the commandant's rose garden. Thankfully, we had both made it away from the scene without our actions being discovered.

"You probably have already guessed this, but I will say it anyway, you're damn lucky it didn't break. Just try to keep as much weight off it as possible for the next week or ten days."

"Yes, doctor," he intoned, with a mock seriousness that changed in a moment. "Mr. Holmes, I've received a communication that said you are fully in the know regarding my activities. As I feared, this appears to be far more than a simple robbery. Can you help me?"

Holmes stood up and began to pace back and forth. "The night of the robbery, who was in residence?"

Toby closed his eyes for a moment, as if letting his mind go back three weeks. "Myself, Creighton and the cook. I had given the other servants the night off. "

"Your man Creighton has been long in your service?" Holmes asked.

"I hired him on only a few years ago. He retired from the army at the same time as I. He had no family, so I offered him a position in my household, which he accepted."

"I take it he worked with you on certain other matters."

"Correct. It was Creighton who discovered the sword was missing. He was making his usual early morning inspection of the house, a habit he has carried over from the army. He was a sergeant major and would inspect his men's bivouac every morning, rain or shine. Trust me on this, Creighton did not miss a spec of dirt on a rifle or uniform button that was out of place.

"It was just after seven, apparently, when he entered the room and discovered that the display case was empty. Nothing else was disturbed and the room was locked, as it is every night," finished Toby.

"While time and human nature may have swept them away, there may yet remain information in that room that could be discerned and might cast light into the darkness that surrounds the events. What did you do when you were informed of the theft?" I knew that look on Holmes' face; he was onto something but only he knew what it was.

"I came at once and searched the room as carefully as I could, being as surprised as I think Creighton was to discover that only the single katana was missing. It actually was not the most valuable item in the collection."

"That is interesting."

A short time later Creighton took us to what Toby referred to as "The Japanese Room."

The room itself was located on the west side of the house and, from the design, I suspected had once actually been two rooms, the modifications made to accommodate the senior Black's extensive collection.

There were free-standing display cases, bookcases, framed items, elegant chairs and curtains along with fans. Whoever had designed the room had an excellent eye for detail. It did not appear to be overcrowded, yet there was not an inch that did not compliment the rest of the room to let visitors relish this unique collection. There had been a lot of time and thought gone into the whole matter.

Holmes had his magnifying lens out and began a through examination of the room. His attention turned at once to the small display case just to the left of the door, now empty, where the katana had been displayed. Over the next two hours I saw him lay flat on the floor, stretch on his toes to examine the tops of the cases, lean halfway out a window. I knew better than to ask for an update on what he was discovering; that information would come when he was ready to release it.

"Watson, we may be in luck. In spite of the passage of so many days and the herd of people who have passed through this area, as I had hoped, there still remains material that is relevant to this matter," he said, holding up several threads along with a round metal disk that he found lodged between a display case and the floor. "This is definitely not a carpenter's shim and may be the thief's calling card."

"Nice of him to leave it. I presume that we are referring to a man?" There had been several rumors in the popular press of a woman cat burglar, though I tended to suspect that she was nothing more than a fantasy dreamed up by some overly imaginative reporter.

"This is definitely not a carpenter's shim and may be the thief's calling card."

"A woman, perhaps, but more than likely a man." He stood over the display case and indicated the edges of it. "If you look closely you will find that the case has been carefully returned to its original state, but not precisely. The locks are just slightly askew from where they should be. The windows also show signs of someone having entered through them, scuff marks that are indicative of someone standing on the sill and coming in from the outside," he said. "It's a pity that the staff is so efficient and keeps the room spotless. But such is life; we must work with what we have."

A few minutes later Holmes had dispatched one of the household staff to the local village to send six telegrams that he had prepared.

"Your pardon, Dr. Black, but I was wondering one thing. Japanese swords such as the stolen one usually come in sets of three, but you have only the one, the katana. Why is that?"

"Quite true, Mr. Holmes, but my father was never able to acquire the matching two, although I know he tried for a number of years," said Toby. "Did you find anything? Anything at all?"

"I found a few indications that convince me that the theft was committed by a professional. Someone, I suspect, may have been hired to do it. The fact that the burglar took only the sword while there was an enormous amount of other items in that room alone that would have been worth thousands of pounds, suggests from the start that he was after only one item."

Toby reached over and put the cigarette he had in his hand into the tray to one side of his chair. A line of smoke lifted up, bending in a slight direction toward the open window.

"Are you suggesting that whoever has the other two swords wanted that one, as well? But why has it been used to kill my two colleagues?"

"That is still an open question, my good doctor, one that I hope to have an answer for soon."

✳

Late in the afternoon, Holmes headed into town to see if he had received answers to his telegrams. Toby and I spent some time reminiscing about our time in the service. But, eventually, I found myself needing to stretch my legs and clear my head, while he dealt with matters about the estate. There are moments when one who has walked abroad in a theater of war needs to be with someone who has shared the experience, and there are equally moments when you do not wish to be around anyone.

I was headed toward the river with the idea of looking it over in advance of a future fishing trip to the area. Toby had already invited Holmes and myself back to partake of the river's bounty once this whole sword business was taken care of.

After a quarter hour of walking I found myself at a bend in the river looking down at the water from some twenty feet above. Even as the light was fading I could make out any number of fish cutting through the water. Looking about I found myself estimating where along the shore would make the best place from which to cast a line.

For a good while I stood there just watching it.

I was about to turn back to the house when I looked down and noticed that my watch had slipped out of my pocket and lay on the ground a few feet away from me. I stooped over to retrieve it when I heard the distinct sound of a rifle shot. It struck the ground only steps away from me.

Without thought I dropped and rolled hard to my left, pushing myself toward the shelter of several trees and low slung bushes. Had I gone to the right I would have plunged over the edge of the cliff and into the river. It struck me just then how ironic it would have been for Holmes to have escaped death at the Reichenbach only to return and have me drown in a river.

I lay still for several minutes, but there were no follow-up shots. It occurred to me that there was every chance it could have been a hunter's shot accidently gone astray. That was what I wanted to believe, but in the pit of my stomach I was convinced that I had been the target of an assassin.

After a few minutes I began to belly crawl across the grass, my goal being a pile of stones waist high ten feet away, not the world's greatest protection, but in these circumstances any protection was better than what I had.

As the shadows lengthened I waited for the attack to continue, but nothing happened. Only the sound of the wind, the river and the forest was around me. After what was actually no more than a few minutes but felt like centuries, I pulled myself up, using the rocks for as much cover as possible. When no other shots rang out I took to my heels and plunged back into the forest.

"Watson, it seems we are making progress."

Sherlock Holmes had spent nearly an hour examining the area where

I had been shot at. We had returned there as the sun was coming up; we had been forced to wait for dawn because of a sudden storm in the middle of the night.

"The elements themselves seem determined to add difficulties to this case." I said.

Following his usual thoroughness, Holmes had even lowered himself slightly over the edge of the small cliff in order to give himself a more exhaustive picture of the area. After he had satisfied himself that there was nothing more to be learned from the edge of the river he led me back towards the far woods, pausing every few minutes to look around and assure himself that he was still on course to whatever point he had determined as the location where the shooter had stood.

"Really, Holmes. I can hardly envision the circumstances where my being shot would constitute progress," I argued.

"But of course it does, old friend. In and of itself, the attempt on your life is genuine proof that our very presence in the area has made someone quite, quite nervous."

"But it could have been just an accidental shot, a hunter taking aim one last time as the sun was going down," I pointed out.

"Possible, but not likely. I believe this is what I am looking for," he pointed with his walking stick at a sturdy-looking pine, not as tall as the others around it, but still topping ten feet in height. The area around it was muddy, a good thorough rain storm had moved through during the night leaving a sea of mud where the grass had not taken hold.

"Yes, here is where he stood." Holmes ran his hand along one of the branches of the tree. "I should judge that he was well over six feet and was right handed."

I arched an eyebrow.

He would deny it, but I have always been convinced that Sherlock Holmes has a strong streak of the music hall performer in him. He loves being the center of attention, especially when it comes to explaining how he has seemingly read someone's mind or discerned some fact about a scene without any apparent help.

"Last night's rain has obscured much evidence, such as footprints which would have given more exacting evidence as to the perpetrators' height and weight. Look here at this branch; there are several marks on it that lead me to believe that your attacker steadied his weapon here.

"The location of the branch and the stance that holding a rifle requires gives me an idea of how tall the man might be. He chose the spot carefully;

this is an older tree and the branch was sturdy enough to hold still while he planned his shot. It is only by happenstance, Watson, that you are still here. Unfortunately, I can find little else to give me information beyond the fact that the man has obviously had some experience using a rifle and has no compunction about taking a human life."

"Is this the work of the thief?" I asked.

Holmes did not speak. He leaned over and picked up several small partially crushed wildflowers. For a long time he seemed to be considering matters.

"I should say the chances are slim. I am coming to the conclusion that we are dealing with two men, perhaps the thief and the man who employed him. There is not enough data to theorize on that aspect of these matters.

"Hear me now, Watson, matters are fast proving to be far more dark and dangerous than a simple robbery. We are entering the dark alleyways and shadowy rooms that my brother spends his life inhabiting, and we must be on our guard to make certain that we are able to emerge again into the sunshine."

As we turned and headed back for the Black home, Holmes reached into his inside pocket and removed several telegrams. "There are several professional thieves who I believe could pull off the kind of robbery we have stumbled into. The problem is, most of them are accounted for. The inquiries I dispatched yesterday have resulted in almost no information. I believe it will be necessary for us to return to London. I must consult someone who is even more familiar with the criminal underclass than I."

"Inspectors Lestrade and Gregson? Or perhaps your brother?"

"Both of the inspectors are good men. I have every respect for them, though they can, as all of their profession, be a little hard-headed and stubborn. No, they were not who I was referring to. As for my brother and the other members of the inner circle of that establishment of his, were it something to do with the dark corridors of politics or espionage, then I would go and speak with him. No, my friend, it is time to pay a call on Col. Sebastian Moran," said Sherlock Holmes.

"What makes you think that Moran will even be willing to talk to you, let alone supply you with that sort of information?"

Holmes had remained silent though much of our return to London. The thing was, during that trip, try as I might, I could conceive of no circumstances under which Moran might agree to assist us. After all, he had been in prison for several months now and it was thanks to Holmes that he was being brought to book for the murder of the Honorable Ronald Adair last April.

"The thief who broke into Black's home was good, very good. I will admit to his being one of the best that I have crossed paths with. I doubt there would have been more evidence remaining had we been on the scene within hours of the theft. Unfortunately, the inquiries I made by telegram did not yield his identity. So it follows that if he is that good, he would more than likely have, at some point or the other, been in the employ of the Moriarty cartel, or at least would have been known to them. I am convinced that Moran will know who we are looking for."

"Possibly, but you still have to convince him to talk. Wouldn't some of his minions do as well and perhaps be more inclined to speak, especially if you threaten their liberty?"

"There would be the matter of locating them and applying the right pressure. Since Moran's arrest, a goodly number have gone to ground. It is time that we have little of, since I fear that matters may soon be coming to a head. So we must try to squeeze the information out of their leader," Holmes elaborated.

It was just after noon when we found ourselves in one of the interrogation rooms in Highgate Prison.

When the warders brought Moran before us, his wrists and ankles chained, he paused in the doorway when he realized who was waiting for him. I swear that for just a moment I saw the hint of a smile on his face. It was a grim self-satisfied thing that vanished as quickly as I was aware of it.

"Come to gloat, have you?" he said, taking a seat in the chair across the table from us. One of the guards disappeared out the door, but the other lingered, stepping back to allow us the illusion of privacy.

For several minutes not a word was uttered; the two men just stared at each other, each taking the other's measure. Though I had never hunted during my time on the Indian subcontinent, watching this scene I had the impression of two great cats who were circling each other, watching for any kind of weakness in their opponent.

Finally, Holmes removed his cigarette case from his inside pocket, took one out, lit it and pushed the case, along with matches, across the table toward Moran. Professor Moriarty's second-in-command eyed it, then reached over and picked up the case, his shackled hands manipulating it quickly and with ease.

"Colonel Moran, let me get to the point. I am here this afternoon seeking your assistance in a matter that has come before me," Holmes began.

Moran held his cigarette between two fingers and began to laugh. It was a loud terrifying sound made even more sinister by the echoes that came from the walls around us.

"Are you telling me, sir, that there is something that the great Mr. Sherlock Holmes does not know, something so important that he has to come to me for assistance?"

"Yes, Colonel, there are a number of things that I do not know. You have only to ask Dr. Watson; he has made that abundantly clear in several of his scribblings."

It wasn't that he didn't know things, it was more that there were a number of subjects in which Holmes had no interest. He knew well where to find the information that he needed for his practice. I had compiled my list of his lack of knowledge and included it in my first novel. That had been published as "A Study in Scarlet." For the record, that was not my title but rather one suggested by my good friend, Dr. Arthur Doyle, over the list of possible ones that I had compiled. He said his would get the readers' attention. In hindsight I must admit to his being correct.

"So why should I help you? After all, it was your interfering in my affairs that has ended with me sleeping behind these walls rather than in my rooms in Justain Street."

"Not to mention facing the possibility of doing a dance with Jack Ketch," added Holmes. "I note that you do not deny the charges facing you. I commend you for that. Know then that, should you assist me by answering the questions I have, I will make it known to the crown prosecutor. I suspect it might make a difference whether he will ask for the death penalty or some lesser sentence when you are found guilty, as I know you will be."

Moran half rose out of his chair, bending toward Holmes. Both the guard and myself moved to interfere, but we were waved away by my friend. Moran continued to stare and then dropped back into his seat.

"I make no promises, let me hear what you want," he said.

"Understand me; I could find the information that I need, but it would take time and that is something I do not have in abundance. Using you as a source of information is a convenience, nothing more. But if I should discover that you deliberately misinform me, I will also make that known to the crown prosecutor, since this matter has implications on a number of government levels. Not to mention, while there are a number of residents behind bars who hate me, there are a number who owe me favors and would be willing to fulfill a request from me."

"I don't react well to threats, Holmes."

"Who said I was making a threat?"

Moran sat silently. Holmes seemed to take that as an agreement to continue.

"Very well. I need a name from you. A second-story man who is good enough to enter a house and leave it without disturbing the residents and to get inside a locked case and take the time to, quite expertly, re-lock the case after removing the contents."

"That would be half the cracksmen in London. You'll have to give me more information than that. You could start with Monteleone, Ochse, Navarro or even Ketchum."

"The first two have been in custody at Scotland Yard for the last six weeks. I know them not to be creative enough to break out, do a job, and then sneak back into prison. Ketchum is in Sweden; I have confirmed that. As for Navarro, he died a month ago; you should keep up with your sources of information." Holmes produced an envelope and laid out the small silver medallion that he had found in the Japanese Room of Black House.

Moran scooped it up and rolled the medallion in his hand. "I believe you are well known for insisting that your clients give you all the facts. You, sir, were withholding information from me. This little gee-gaw gives me the name that you are needing. I just want your word that you will do as you say." The former assistant to Professor Moriarty for once seemed to be sincere.

"If you know me at all, you know I am a man of my word."

"That will be your undoing one day. But the name you are looking for is one that I cannot say even exists. Mad Jack Moore. The professor tried to recruit him, but he declined."

"Someone declined Moriarty? I am impressed. However, I have hard rumors of this cracksman but nothing that actually proves he is more than a legend. Where do I find him?"

"That, I don't know. But I do know someone who does. Have you ever heard of Auntie Gwendolyn?" asked Moran. "They say that if a rat farts in Soho she will know about it within an hour and be willing to sell the information within two. The word I had was that if you wanted to hire Mad Jack, you talked to Auntie Gwendolyn."

"Thank you, Colonel," Holmes said, rising. "I shall keep my promise and report your cooperation to the proper authorities."

"Go to hell," said Moran.

Ж

"So where do we find this Auntie Gwendolyn?" I asked.

The carriage had dropped us off near Speakers' Corner in Hyde Park. There were the usual numbers of street corner speechmakers holding forth on every subject from taxes to legalized prostitution to how obvious it was, according to one person, that the spirits of the dead were walking among us. In other words, everything was perfectly normal for Hyde Park.

"This is one of a number of places that make an excellent spot to observe and learn about humanity," said Holmes. "I recall when I was young and would come down to London to stay with brother Mycroft, he and I would come here. It helped me to hone my skills of observation."

One thing that I had noticed since his return was that Holmes had become occasionally more effusive about his past. I suspect that when you are three years away from every aspect of your previous life you become a bit nostalgic, though for Holmes, that seemed almost a contradiction in terms.

He led us to a far southern corner of the park where an older woman was selling flowers. Some that she had in pails and on her cart I strongly suspected might have come from graves in several local cemeteries, but since that didn't seem to bother Holmes, and obviously had not incurred the wrath of the police, I said nothing.

"And what can I do for you fine gentlemen? Something perhaps to take home to add a bit of color to your study or to entice that all important smile from a lady? I have some fresh roses that would do the trick." The woman had one of the worst cases of halitosis that I had ever encountered. It was a complete wonder to me that the flowers around her did not wilt away when she breathed on them.

"No, I would, however, be interested in an orchid; it is for my Aunt Gwendolyn," said Holmes. He laid ten pence on her cart, formed in a triangle pointing at her. The woman looked at them for a moment, then looked at Holmes who then casually moved three of them to where the triangle was perfect reversed and pointing back at him.

The woman muttered to herself as she looked over several of her flower pails, then turned back to us and shrugged. "I 'm afraid that I can't accommodate you; I sold the last of those not a half hour ago to Lord

Rocklynne."

"Thank you, madam. May the rest of the day bring you much business."

We were a hundred yards away from her before I spoke. "I am presuming that little exchange had more to do with locating Mad Jack Moore than it did with horticulture."

"It did, indeed. The woman is one of Moriarty's minions. If you know the proper way of asking, she will send you where you need to go. In this case it is to Auntie Gwendolyn who is sitting on that bench," Holmes raised his walking stick and pointed at a park bench fifty feet away from us.

For the life of me I would have sworn that the man sitting on the bench, tossing handfuls of feed out to the pigeons was the same old bookseller who had barged into my consulting room two months ago and turned out to be Holmes, himself, in disguise.

"I see where you get your ideas for disguises," I commented.

Holmes ignored me and sent the pigeons flying. He strode up to the park bench.

"A good day to you," Holmes addressed the man. "I'm told that you would be Aunt Gwendolyn."

"I'm who I need to be, sir. If you need a copy of 'The White Company,' I can supply that, as well," the man replied.

"Thank you, but no," continued Holmes. "I possess a signed first edition. I was directed to you by Colonel Sebastian Moran. He seemed to think that you could supply me with the information that I need."

The old man nodded. "That you were able to speak to him says volumes. What can I do for you?"

"I need to locate a cracksman, one Mad Jack Moore. I also need to know who he most recently received a commission from. If you can supply that information as well, that would be excellent; if not, I will ask him directly."

The old man chewed his lip for a moment. "Mad Jack keeps rooms on Montague Street, though it won't do you any good to go there. As of yesterday, he had not been seen in over a month. The last I knew, he had taken a commission to acquire some sort of fancy foreign knife. The problem is that four days after Jack left to 'acquire' them I heard that the person who was hiring him dropped dead of a heart attack while he was walking into Parliament."

When I heard that I searched my memory for the name of anyone who had died on the steps of Parliament, but could remember nothing. I had not been paying as close attention to the newspapers as I knew that Holmes did.

"The thing was he was supposed to be back within three days. That was weeks ago and our Jack is, shall we say, a creature of habit when he is not involved in his work. He's in and out and back home before you can blink an eye."

"Could he have chosen to decamp to foreign climes?" asked Holmes.

"That's highly doubtful," said Auntie Gwendolyn. "He did a bit of roving when he were younger, but ten years ago swore he would never leave this island again. Something out there scared him, something he would never talk about even to his 'untie.' That's why he started asking me to set up his business appointments."

That was when things got a little strange. As if talking to a man called Auntie Gwendolyn wasn't strange enough, the man began to recite a series of nonsense words, like something from a mad poet's word bag. This did not deter Holmes; he laid his hand on the man's shoulder and gently shook it until he seemed to notice him again.

"Is there anything else?"

"Are you certain that Jack did not stumble onto a new job, perhaps something that he saw or someone that he talked to while he was fetching the sword up north?" asked Holmes.

"You know about the sword?" Our man seemed genuinely surprised by that. He glanced around furtively. "Don't mention it to anyone. Jack doesn't even know who it is what wants the sword, just that someone does and they were willing to pay for the best, and that's our Jackie boy."

"But could he have found another job while doing this one?"

Auntie Gwendolyn scratched his stubble-covered chin for a moment, then grabbed a handful of crumbs and scattered it out in front of him. The pigeons dove for it like hungry wolves. "Anyone else, I would say yes, he could have stumbled onto something that piqued his interest and promised to make a dime or two. But not our Mad Jack. That is a fact that you can take to the bank today and it will be solid gold a year from now."

"Thank you, Auntie Gwendolyn."

It was perfectly obvious, even to me, that no one had been in the rooms that Mad Jack Moore maintained in Montague Street for quite some time. There was a layer of dust on everything and the air hung stale and warm. A five pound note to the landlord was effective a key as the well-worn set of picklocks that I knew that Holmes had in one of his pockets.

I spotted several partially full lacquered bottles sitting on top of a dresser. Holmes looked at them for a moment, then picked one up and took a sniff.

"Bourbon, from Kentucky. This Mad Jack seems to know his liquor and is not afraid to pay for it."

"Either that, or its part of the loot from one of his robberies," I observed. "Does this mean he might be about and that he just hasn't bothered to check in with Auntie Gwendolyn?"

"Not a distinct possibility, Watson. If these were part of the loot from a break-in, it would have to be sometime in the past. No one has cleaned these rooms in some weeks."

As Holmes began to prowl over the room, I began carefully to examine the things that fell within my line of sight. I know there is much to be inferred from even the tiniest detail. As I worked my way around the room I was able to infer a number of things: that Jack Moore seemed to like a particular newspaper. There were numerous copies of one of the less well-known Fleet Street periodicals, the kind that sell for a half penny, and you feel that you have been overcharged. I had looked at it on occasion, myself, and will only say that it was obvious that the journalists—and I use that term quite, quite loosely—had extremely vivid imaginations. However, I elevated my ideas of Mad Jack's literary tastes when I found a number of copies of The Strand magazine near the bed, several of them including my accounts of Holmes' work.

"We don't have time for you to remind yourself of how fancifully you presented our past cases, Doctor," admonished Holmes.

I didn't ask him how he knew what I was looking at, since my back was to him. The fact that he recognized the covers and knew the contents was not one that was lost on me. I have learned a thing or two over the years from my association with my old friend.

"If I knew what we were looking for, I might be able to speed things up."

"If I knew, I would tell you," he said. "I think…."

Holmes stopped in the middle of the sentence and grabbed up a sheaf of three pages that had been impaled on the top of one of those cheap replicas of the Eiffel tower that far too many tourists bring back from France.

"Yes," he said, half muttering the word. "This is everything that I was hoping for. Come, Watson, the game is on!"

𝕏

The "official" office assigned to Mycroft Holmes, in his position as an auditor of the books of government departments, was a small one located in the basement of a building occupied by one of the more obscure governmental ministries. However, it was not the place where he actually 'worked,' as his brother explained to me.

"I sincerely doubt that he has been in that place more than a dozen times in the last couple of years," said Sherlock Holmes. "I was actually quite surprised when he replied to my telegram to meet him there."

After completing our search of Mad Jack Moore's quarters, Holmes had insisted that we walk several blocks before flagging down a hansom cab.

"I don't think that Mad Jack was being watched, but this was a way to make certain of it," he said once we had boarded the cab.

"So was it? And were we followed?"

"If we were, they were good enough that I saw nothing," was the only reply that he made.

There was a very musty smell in the air as we arrived at the series of small dark offices that filled the lower floor of the ministry. I noticed several men in one of the other offices, conferring over three large account books. They seemed to be trying to match up what was written on some papers with the ledgers, and from the looks on their faces I suspected that they were not having much success in the matter.

Mycroft Holmes' office was small and cramped, with barely enough room for his desk, a filing cabinet and a pair of gas lights on either wall that seemed to do more to make shadows than to dispel them. There was a man standing next to Mycroft's desk, his half spectacles hanging on the end of his nose.

"The case from the warehouse is to go to the British Museum; see to it personally that it is handed over to the curator of the rare manuscripts department. If for any reason he is not there, take it to the castle, instead."

"At once, Mr. Holmes," he said.

"Come in, Sherlock. Come in, Dr. Watson. I'm afraid that this is not as comfortable as a meeting at the Diogenes Club, but circumstances demand my presence in the building right now. The situation in Bavaria has become somewhat unstable."

I took the chair to the right of his desk while Holmes remained standing. "I'm surprised that you could find your way down here, Mycroft. You still keeping the Cuban cigars in that hollowed-out copy of British Birds?"

"You're the consulting detective. Detect," he smiled. The two brothers might have issues with each other, but even in the sparring I could see the

Holmes had insisted that we walk several blocks before flagging down a hansom cab.

genuine affection that these two men had for each other.

"We don't have the time. I need to know something about your man, Black," said Holmes. "What did he and the other two do in Japan?"

"I never said that Black, Goldman and Malone worked together in Japan."

"Please, Mycroft. Don't insult my intelligence; that's why the two were killed, and with the same weapon. A weapon you feared would be used against Black. Is it as revenge for what they did there? Otherwise, why would you have called me into the case and been so ardent that I take it on?"

Mycroft Holmes had a look of irritation on his face. "I dislike rehashing past events, especially ones that did not work the way I had honestly hoped they would. You understand that there is a great deal that I cannot tell you. It was five years ago and certain aspects of the matter are still in flux and could cause a great deal of embarrassment to the government, as well as certain people in other countries who have made themselves available to us."

"Naturally, Mycroft, you know that neither Watson nor I will breathe a word of the matter. Remember, it was you who asked the two of us to get involved. Showing loyalty and trying to protect the people who have worked for you is most commendable, and, knowing you, the expected thing to do."

"Let us say that Black, Goldman and Malone went into Japan with the intention of setting up an intelligence network. There are certain factions in Japan who, should they come to power, could potentially represent a threat to this country. In spite of the fact that his rule is supposed to be absolute, the emperor has been, at times, under the thumb of factions who are not friendly to Great Britain," lectured Mycroft Holmes.

"So your people were setting up a sleeper network, something not for current intelligence needs, but for future use, perhaps even hoping that it would never be needed," extrapolated Holmes.

"Exactly. Unfortunately, things fell apart; the three men barely made it out of Japan alive. They had arranged a meeting with a number of officials who were sympathetic to the British cause. 'Others' became aware of it and set the place on fire; killing the loyalists along with the family that lived there. When that sword was stolen and the two men were murdered, I suspected them to be revenge killings. That is why I brought you into the matter."

"And did not give me all the facts. You know that was the equivalent of tying both arms behind me and expecting me to turn cartwheels."

"There is some information, Sherlock, that does not come within the venue of the private detective. It was need-to-know."

"I need to know. Do you have a list of the people who were killed in that fire?"

"I believe so." He began to rummage around the desk, finally pulling out a thick bundle of papers. "Here's the case file."

Holmes grabbed it out of his brother's hands and began tearing through the pages. Finally he found the list of names. He ran his finger down the page and paused at the bottom of it.

"Who was in charge of this operation?" demanded Holmes.

"That would be Dr. Black."

"Then we have little time," said Sherlock Holmes. "Look at the three names at the bottom of the list."

X

The sounds of the river seemed louder than they had the last time that we had been here. When we had departed the area (had it been only two days before?), I had hardly expected that I would see the river or anything in the area any time in the near future. Returning here for the fishing was one of those plans that you make, but never actually get around to. But here we were, and certainly not without the knowledge of my old army companion.

"And we are here, why?" I asked Holmes. This was the third time over the last few hours that I had asked him, and for the third time he remained silent. I could almost hear the connecting gears of his mind rolling, checking and rechecking the facts of this case. I only wish he would share what he knew, because I had the distinct feeling that we were within striking distance of a solution. I just didn't have many ideas of what it might be.

Holmes ranged a dozen steps ahead of me as we approached the river. Our driver sat quietly with his carriage, the two horses pulling it munching away on sacks of feed as he puffed on his pipe, wondering just what two Londoners who had no doubt escaped from Bedlam wanted in this remote village.

"What was on that paper that you found in Moore's quarters?" I asked.

"That was a communication to Mad Jack from his employer, no doubt relayed through Auntie Gwendolyn, setting up a meeting in this area so that Jack could deliver the man's prize directly into his hands," said Holmes.

"And given what happened to Goldman and Malone...."

Holmes finished my thought. "We can extrapolate what more than likely happened to Mad Jack Moore. The chances that we will find the body are slim to none, but it is worth the look. It also said that at all costs he had to have the sword before the twenty-sixth of the month."

"Which he did," I said.

For the next hour he and I scoured the area. Rain, wind and just the passing of time had not been kind to signs of a crime. Not to mention, how could one tell if something might have to do with the break in or was left behind by a passing farmer making his way to the manor house?

I was right. All that time resulted in our finding several mud-encrusted shillings, a crumbled up page from a newspaper dated more than a month before, and a broken piece of watch chain that had been caught in between several low branches.

Holmes took a cigarette from his case, but did not light it. He looked around the landscape, now swept in lengthening shadows as the sun was disappearing into the west.

"It is time, Watson. We shall lay our trap this night."

Once again Holmes had lapsed into his silent mode. Only now we were waiting, hidden in the grove of trees just opposite the Black manor house. After dismissing our driver, Holmes had led me in an indirect route to this observation post.

"Think of it as a tiger trap," he suggested.

Those words echoed much from only a few weeks ago, when he and I had waited in the darkness of the empty house across from Baker Street. At least in this place, in spite of the fact that we were outside, it was a warm summer evening.

There was little activity in the house. I could see Toby moving around inside. In just a couple of days he had become quite good at maneuvering with the crutches.

"Who is the tiger?" I asked. "And isn't it traditional in a matter such as this to have a goat tied out to lure the animal to its destiny?"

"We have," nodded my companion and gestured toward the house.

I was not pleased with the idea that Toby was our bait, but could think of no argument against Holmes' plan. Holmes checked his pocket watch twice in the next little while before motioning for me to follow him.

I had my army revolver in one hand and my medical bag in the other. The contrast, death and healing, did not escape me.

We moved as quickly as possible across the lawn, staying in the darkest shadows until we were at the study window. There was a sudden crash from inside followed by a scream that sounded more bestial than human. Almost immediately Holmes had the window open and was hoisting himself through it.

"The door, Watson! Do not let him past you!"

I wasted no time in heading for the front door. Dropping my bag in the hallway, I blocked the study door.

The scene inside was chaotic at best, what I could see of it. There was a single oil lamp burning at the far end of the room but it barely gave enough light to see that part of the area. I heard something crash into the wall and saw Holmes tumbling onto the floor. A huge figure, bellowing at the top of his lungs, charged at Holmes. The attacker held a sword in his two hands, raised for the attack.

I brought my pistol up and swiftly pulled the trigger, three shots, one after the other, blasting into the attacker. The man shook at the impact; blood flew everywhere, showering Holmes as he came to his feet. His attacker stood stone still, long enough for my friend to tackle him and drive the man down to the ground.

The sword crashed into one of the display cases that held several battle flags and a vase holding flowers.

"Holmes!" I yelled.

"I'm all right. See to Dr. Black!"

It took several seconds for my eyes to focus as I searched the semi-darkness of the room. Tobias Algernon Black lay sprawled on the floor. His smoking jacket was black with blood.

I knelt at his side and touched the side of his neck. The skin was warm and the pulse strong.

"Looks like you get your chance to pay me back for saving your life, Watson," he said as he grimaced in pain.

"Well, Watson," said Holmes, appearing at my side with my medical bag. I fished out bandages and alcohol, along with something for the pain that I knew he was feeling.

"I can't tell for sure, but it looks like he was lucky. The damage is minor, but unless I'm much worse of a doctor than I think I am, I think he will be all right. But it will take a lot longer to get over this than that twisted ankle of his."

"He could have no better doctor at his side than you," said Holmes.

"What about him?" I gestured toward the still form of our attacker.

"Dead. You are still an excellent shot."

I was not happy with my having killed the fellow, but better him than us. "Who is it? Was he the one we were looking for?"

"That he was," Holmes said. He had relit one of the oil lamps and walked over to the body, shining the light on the man's face.

It was Creighton, the butler.

X

I laid the newspaper down on the table next to remnants of Mrs. Hudson's excellent breakfast. From outside the window I could hear the early morning sounds of Baker Street that seemed so familiar and yet so distant.

"It still seems amazing that he was living in the same house with Toby and wanting to kill him all along," I said.

"We've seen it before: an angry wife, a brother who feels he was cheated out of his proper due by his family, a secretary who feels that he has been treated like the mud off his employer's shoe," said Holmes.

Ironically, I could put a case to each of his examples.

"But what set Creighton off? I understand that there was a seething hatred over the death of his sister and his niece in that fire in Japan, though why he did not blame the men who set the fire, rather than Toby and his associates, I don't know."

Holmes took several puffs on his cigarette before setting it down on the edge of the coffee cup. "There we can only enter into the realm of speculation, since Creighton is no longer with us. If you recall, Mycroft mentioned that Malone and Goldman had returned to this country only in the last few months from extended duties overseas. Perhaps they contacted Dr. Black, whether as part of an assignment or simply to renew friendships. As the major domo of the Black household, Creighton would have been in a position to know of it. That, I would say, probably set him off on his quest for revenge."

"Why steal the katana?"

"His sister had married into a Japanese family and they accepted him as part of the family. The blade had at one point belonged to them; I suspect he felt that using it to avenge his sister was a matter of honor."

Toby had described how, that evening, Creighton had appeared in the door of the study, the stolen katana in his hand. He had succeeded in stabbing him, but Toby had evaded the man by the simple act of throwing himself on the floor. That had bought a few moments, but it had been enough for Holmes and myself to appear on the scene.

I took my coffee cup and walked over to my chair near the window. On the table was a photograph of Mary. She never liked it, in fact, saying that she really didn't like any of the photographs that had been taken of her. I, on the other hand, thought then and now it was the most beautiful thing I had ever seen.

I could almost hear her say, "You did well, John."

"For once in his life, my dear brother missed a vitally important piece of information," said Sherlock Holmes. "His confounded plans within plans within plans may save the nation at times, but in this case they almost cost a man his life. Had I seen the file earlier I would have made the connection I needed."

"Are you saying this case wasn't elementary?" I asked.

"You know as well as I; they rarely are," laughed Holmes.

The End

Discovering Sherlock Holmes

I discovered Sherlock Holmes because of the movies and Ellery Queen.

One weekend evening I was bitterly disappointed because the local television station was not going to be showing their regular late night horror movie. Instead it was something called "The Hound of the Baskervilles" and had an actor named Basil Rathbone playing this detective named Sherlock Holmes.

Let's just say I was up way too late watching every minute of it and the next day asking my dad, who had been in the movie theatre business all his life, if there were any more.

Not long thereafter I wandered into a purveyor of paperbacks and happened to notice a new book by my then favorite mystery writer, Ellery Queen. I didn't know it at the time but it wasn't an original novel but rather a novelization of a movie, "A Study in Terror" that featured Sherlock Holmes vs. Jack the Ripper. I devoured that book, which still sits on my bookshelf to this day, and soon discovered the original stories by Doyle as well as the tales that others had written about the residents of 221B Baker Street.

Over the years, during which I started writing and publishing stories myself, I began toying with an idea of writing one myself. I eventually did, "The Adventure of the Other Detective," but with my inclinations it had a major science fictional twist.

That story—set in October, 1894, a few months after Holmes' return from his alleged death at the hands of Moriarity—followed a tradition that Watson was well known for, mentioning of other cases that were never published: such as the disappearance of the ship Alicia, the matter of Ricoletti of the Club Foot and, of course, the Giant Rat of Sumatra among others. So I decided to have Watson mention several cases that had not, at the time, been presented to the public, for reasons both delicate and scandalous: "The Theft of Alhazred's Manuscript,' The Adventure of the

Black Katana" and "The Quest for Pendragon's Sun."

"The Adventure of the Black Katana" is the second of those tales to actually see print. In none of the original tales from Doyle do you ever hear any mention of the men that Watson served with in the Army; this gave me a chance to show a bit more of his background. I also wanted to show that it took Watson time to get over the loss of his beloved Mary.

There will, of course be more tales of Mr. Sherlock Holmes and his good friend Dr. John Hamish Watson, both from my pen and others because "The game is (and always will be) afoot."

BRADLEY H. SINOR has seen his work appear in numerous science fiction, fantasy and horror anthologies such as *The Improbable Adventures Of Sherlock Holmes, Tales Of The Shadowmen, The Grantville Gazette And Ring Of Fire* 2 and 3. Three collections of his short fiction have been released by Yard Dog Press, *Dark And Stormy Nights, In The Shadows,* and *Playing With Secrets* (along with stories by his wife Sue Sinor.) His newest collections are *Echoes From The Darkness* (Arctic Wolf Press) and *Where The Shadows Began* (Merry Blacksmith Press). He can be reached via his wall on Facebook.

Sherlock Holmes

in

"The Adventure of the Anonymous Heiress"

By
William R. Thinnes

*I*n my endeavor to chronicle the various exploits of my friend Mr. Sherlock Holmes, I have, over these several years, set down for my readers a number of unique instances which afforded my companion exercise of his considerable talents for observation, inference and deduction in the service of solving crimes and bizarre happenstance. My readers will be familiar with some of the occasions, where they have been released to the public according to the wise judgement or, as often, whim of Sherlock Holmes. He has, however, frequently deemed certain of his cases unsuitable for publication, owing either to the private nature of the matter, or to unwieldy or fantastic particulars which cry out for explanation or elaboration, but which, indeed, cannot be explained or elaborated upon. The problem of the fisherman's net and the albatross; the parakeet that only sang at midnight; the peculiar affair of the mute headmaster; these are but a handful of that masterful detective's adventures which cannot, at least for the present, see light of day nor printer's ink.

The following narrative stood squarely with these until just recently, when the principal involved, along with Holmes, gave me permission to put upon paper this most unusual and, at times, grotesque example of my friend's analytical prowess.

It was late in the autumn of 1887. The stifling swelter of summer had ended and London's streets were beginning to feel the crisp chill of approaching winter. The few trees lining Baker Street were already bare of leaves, and the street sweeps had long since borne them away.

Holmes and I, comfortably ensconced at that time in our lodgings at 221B Baker Street, had finished our breakfast and were taking our morning leisure. My friend, with his long legs stretched out before him and slumped down on the sofa, clasped his hands under his chin and gazed abstractedly toward the ceiling. I sat at my sturdy oaken desk and was attempting to catch up on a bit of the latest medical findings; I had been neglecting my practice somewhat of late and was feeling guilty.

There was a fire in the hearth to take the nip out of the morning air, courtesy of Mrs. Hudson, our persevering landlady, and Holmes, as he slouched before it in mouse-colored dressing gown and slippers, had that languorous expression on his face that I had come to associate with his lamentable use of cocaine, a substance he took solace in during periods of inactivity or boredom, states of being he loathed with all of his bohemian soul.

A substance, also, that he had given me reason to believe he had—grudgingly, to be sure!—relinquished. This last due to my concern for Holmes' physical well-being and, moreover, to my persistent badgering of the man. I believed I had helped wean my astute companion from the noxious stuff. Was I mistaken? When next I chanced to look up from my medical journal Holmes was toying with a revolver, squinting down its polished barrel and idly waving it about. Then at last he leveled it at the wall next to the sideboard and steadied the hand that held it.

"Holmes!" I cried. "Surely we can do without another bulletpocked paean to Her Majesty! Our long-suffering landlady has not quite got over your last burst of patriotism."

He sat examining the weapon for another moment. "A hair-trigger, Watson. Totally unsuitable, due to its delicate mechanism, for anything save trick-shooting. I took this away from one of our great city's break-in professionals, although I admit the purpose to which he would put this curio eludes me."

He looked down the barrel again, arm outstretched. "Just the merest pressure and..."

"Holmes!"

He laughed gaily, gave me a wink, and jumped up to place the offending weapon on the mantle, then filled his long cherrywood pipe with tobacco from the Persian slipper hanging nearby. It was a foul Turkish blend, which he lit and puffed merrily as he crossed the room and plopped down upon the sofa once again.

"My dear fellow, is that an air of crotchetiness overtaking your usually amiable persona?" He smiled at me, eyes twinkling. "As for the cocaine, you need not fear that I have reneged on my assurances to no longer partake, although I do confess a longing for it when things bog down here. Life has not been half so interesting since our friend Moriarty left this earthly abode."

He sent a plume of dark grey smoke toward the ceiling with that, and slid further down into the embrace of the couch.

I was startled by his reference to cocaine. "My dear sir, how in heaven's name did you fathom that I was thinking of that drug! I made no mention...."

"Tut, tut, Watson! But you did mention it. Your eyes proclaimed it when, upon seeing me in my little reverie, they darted to that portion of the mantle where formerly I kept my syringe-box." His tone was low and grave, but his eyes glittered as he spoke. As always, once Holmes had explained his little feat of what had appeared to be mental telepathy of some sort, his observation appeared simple to the extreme. Holmes enjoyed these little parlor tricks; he had more than a dash of the showman in him. Suddenly the detective leapt up from the sofa, walked swiftly to a small table by the door and picked up a telegram, waving it gently in the air.

"I received this last evening. We are due for a visitor shortly, a young woman, if I'm not mistaken. From her rather terse missive I gather we will soon have a problem to consider, for she communicates she is at her wit's end. Have you anything of a pressing nature this morning? I would judge not. If that is so, I would welcome your presence when she calls upon us. Twelve sharp, or so says her note."

※

It was only a minute short of noon when the estimable Mrs. Hudson knocked upon our door, informing us of our visitor's arrival.

"Show her up, if you please," said Holmes, as I drew up a chair across from our own and near the fire for our lady-in-distress.

A moment later a young woman of perhaps twenty entered our apartment, ushered through the portal by our landlady. Dressed in the latest women's fashions—but not in an extravagant or gaudy manner—her apparel bespoke taste and, perhaps, a certain conservatism. Her visage was comely and fair, but for the faint trace of dark circles beneath her wide green eyes. Her auburn hair was cut fairly short beneath her wide bonnet. As she took our hands in turn to greet us, I could not help but notice that her own shook visibly.

"Pray be seated, Miss Sectate," said Holmes with a wave to the chair. The young lady fell into the proffered object with a pronounced sigh. Her anguished eyes darted for a moment between Holmes' face and mine, searching, I thought, for a sign of warmth or sympathy. She apparently found it, for after a moment a touch of color rose in her cheek and her hands ceased worrying at her bag.

"Oh, what an awful business!" She blurted out suddenly, startling me.

I glanced at Holmes; he sat appraising our new acquaintance with fingertips together at his chin, eyelids lowered, his mien one of calm and concentration.

Our visitor went on: "It has been too much for me of late, and I did not know to whom to turn. My father spoke of you once, Mr. Holmes; you helped a friend of his in years gone by, and impressed him mightily, and so I thought that, well, perhaps you might come to my aid as well. Peters is not here to…."

"Miss Sectate," Holmes interrupted, "I see that you are in some difficulty and I am prepared to do what I can. However: I would have you begin at the beginning. If I am to be of service I must know everything. Ah, Mrs. Hudson, some hot tea for our guest. Thank you. And so! Your journey from North Sussex was, I trust, amenable?"

"Yes, the trip was…" she began, then halted and looked at my companion who had perhaps the faintest trace of a smile at his lips. "How could you know that? I mentioned nothing of my residence in Sussex in my telegram!" Her green eyes widened somewhat alarmingly.

For some reason, I was, at that moment, struck with the rather unique beauty of the young lady. Allowed for a moment to step out of the shadows of her troubles and worry, she radiated a feisty sort of intelligence and demeanor that suited her well.

Holmes relit his pipe and looked at our visitor frankly. "Permit me. I observe upon the hem of your dress faint indications of a yellow-brownish mud, possibly engendered by a passing hansom or dog-cart. As Watson can testify, I am no little authority on the various soil types to be found in this country—we will not speak of elsewhere—and have published a monograph on the subject. The type which now mars your skirts is a clay found only in areas of North Sussex and near Liverpool. Your accent infers Sussex rather than the latter, and I therefore deduce that is the district from which you hail."

The young woman's face brightened considerably after this exposition of my friend's talents. "Oh, perhaps you are the man for me! But let me start anew."

"Pray do," encouraged my friend, and we settled back in our chairs attentively.

"My name, as you know, Mr. Holmes—but perhaps your friend does not—is Julia Sectate. My father is John Sectate, the last of his family. James, my brother and only sibling, died five years ago of pneumonia. We have lived all our lives, as had my father's family before him, in Sectate Manor in—well, you know where it is, don't you! Since my brother and mother, who died when I was very young, are both gone, it has been Father and I and, until recent months, the servants. We are quite well off financially—I say that not in any boastful manner, but in truth—and there is a considerable inheritance which, someday I suppose, must come to me. We live far from the nearest town, which is Kinson, and to speak the truth I have had little association with other people, outside of the family, tutors and servants. Until recently, though, I have not wanted for companionship, as there was my brother, when he was alive, my father and the servants' children for society."

Here Miss Sectate paused at length, looking down at her lap and gently biting her lower lip. After half a minute passed, Holmes stated, "Pray continue," and there was a small measure of impatience in his tone.

Miss Sectate gathered her thoughts and went on: "When Jim died it was a crushing blow for both my father and me, but Father took it exceptionally hard and fell into a deep despair. I mean, it was hard under any circumstances, but—well, Jim was his only son, the last male in the Sectate line...."

"We understand," I murmured.

"Six months ago Father became quite ill. For reasons I still do not comprehend, he dismissed all the servants, save for a solitary caretaker, Peters...."

"Tell me about this Peters," interjected Holmes.

"Peters was an odd little man, rather eccentric, but very nice. He was very taken with astrology, tarot cards and the like. Superstitious. He used to read me my horoscope, tell me my future. I didn't believe in it, but it was amusing. He was very kind to me."

"'Was,'" said Sherlock Holmes. "You speak of him in the past tense. Why? What has happened to the man?"

"I am coming to that. What is more terrible is that the doctor says Father has gone steadily downhill these last few months, and now is not expected to live out the week." At this juncture Miss Sectate began to quietly weep, and her shoulders shook convulsively with her sobbing.

Holmes arose and placed his hand on our caller's arm. "There, there," he murmured sympathetically.

After a pause he said, "There are two questions. One: You say that according to the doctor your father's sickness has worsened. Have you not seen your father yourself? And two: What of Peters, the caretaker?"

After some moments the girl looked up at us with overflowing eyes, sniffed softly into her handkerchief, and answered Holmes' queries.

"I have not seen my father for some time, due to the terrible contagion of his illness. The doctor forbids it. As to Peters...oh, Mr. Holmes, so much more has transpired! As if Jim's death and Father's horrible sickness aren't enough for anyone to bear! Two months ago while walking my mare Scilla, I...I came across old Peters, lying at the edge of the garden—gasping for air like a drowning man! It was horrible, horrible...his face all mottled and purple, his arms flailing and hands grabbing at nothing, at the air...l ran to fetch Father's doctor immediately, but before he could do anything for him, Peters babbled a few words and died!"

"Do you recall Peters' words?" asked Holmes abruptly.

"'Jim and I.' Those were his words, as nearly as I could ascertain. I don't know why he would name James, who had passed away five years ago, but those were his words. The doctor examined Peters and told me he had a weak heart, but—"

"But what, Miss Sectate?" I asked.

"I once saw one of the cooks having a heart attack, years ago, and this wasn't the same! Peter's hands were at his throat at times, as if it were burning, or he was choking."

She paused, then gazed firmly at both of us. "I don't believe Peters had a heart attack at all!"

Our visitor paused again, as if gathering her strength about her, then proceeded with her tale. "There is more to tell. The police came and found nothing out of sorts; Peter's death was officially laid to heart failure. I said nothing of my suspicion that that wasn't the cause. What had I to support my feeling? A vague presentiment, intuition? And so I kept silent.

"After the funeral, I advertised for a new caretaker, out of necessity. With the servants gone, and Father deathly ill, I am hardly able to care for the estate myself, and Father, says the doctor, will not budge in rehiring the servants, although I doubt any would care to live in that lonely, contagious atmosphere anyway. There is a lovely, though small, caretaker's cottage on the grounds, however, and apparently Father does not begrudge me that assistance.

"At any rate, a month ago I had a reply to my advertisement, and interviewed the man the following week. He seemed able enough, honest, and had some experience, so I was predisposed to employ him, and when he asked if it would be all right if his wife came to live at the cottage with him, I said most assuredly, yes! I have sorely felt the dearth of feminine companionship since the staff was let go, and more than welcomed the presence of another lady, especially one approximately my own age, as Mrs. Ivers was said to be.

"The man—Ivers is his name, you will have guessed—moved into the cottage immediately with his wife. He has since performed his duties well, and is good about keeping the place up, but has developed an unsavory attitude of late; impatient and rude to his wife, muttering under his breath when I ask him to perform some task or criticize him."

Holmes interrupted her tale. "Why not dismiss him, and find someone more suitable?"

Julia Sectate looked at us with sadness in her eyes. "Alas, I cannot do that, Mr. Holmes, and the reason is his wife: she has become dear to me. We spend nearly every waking moment together, chatting, playing cards, walking about the estate. She asks me thousands of questions about myself, and I, her. We have become the closest of friends at a time when I have been starved for any company at all!"

Holmes sat stock-still in his chair, eyes dreamy and hands in supplication under his chin. "Your story interests me, Miss Sectate, but I must ask this: What do you wish of me?"

The young woman sat stiffly in her seat, eyes welling with tears again, face as pale as when she first entered our rooms. "My story is not yet finished, gentlemen. The event which has spurred me to come to London and seek your counsel is this: two days ago I went to the stables on our estate to take Scilla—my Arabian mare—for her morning ride, as I do every day. She was not in her stall, Mr. Holmes! I searched everywhere for her, but in vain. Later, Ivers told me he had found her body—dead, by the woods that border our land on the south, savaged as if by some wild animal! Ivers informed me a pack of wild dogs has been seen running in the woods and territories thereabouts, and that they probably killed poor, dear Scilla.

"Ivers buried her yesterday, near the stables. Mr. Holmes, there is something dreadfully amiss! Sickness, death, the new caretaker, the servants' dismissals; I feel there is evil on our land, and if you can set my mind at ease concerning these events, I'll be forever in your debt."

Holmes rose, walked to the bay window overlooking Baker Street, and gazed out distractedly for a minute. One could hear the clatter of horses' hooves and the rattle of hansoms from the byway below.

Then he returned abruptly and spoke. "We will look into this matter, Miss Sectate, and if there is anything sinister afoot we will do our best to put it right."

Turning to me, he said, "Watson, how would you fancy a sojourn to Sussex? The air is crisp and clear, and I imagine the countryside looks quite fetching this time of the year."

The young lady turned to my friend and impulsively put her arms out as if to embrace him. Holmes gave a strange smile and stepped back with hand raised in front of him. Miss Sectate desisted, but smiled upon us.

"Oh, thank you, thank you, Mr. Holmes! You are a kind man, and I feel a great relief already. I have in the future considerable money coming to me, and some little put away at present, so…"

Holmes interrupted her. "…We can discuss those particulars later; what I require now are precise directions to Sectate Manor. We shall leave from Charing Cross this afternoon. Watson, if you would be so kind as to consult the railway tables…."

X

And so we found ourselves bound for Sussex on the two-fifteen from Charing Cross. I spent much of the journey mildly engrossed in a yellow-backed novel. Holmes, attired in a long coat and cap to ward off the chill of early November, sat with his chin buried in his chest, apparently deep in thought and seemingly oblivious to the gorgeous fall countryside rushing past us. Before our client had departed Holmes had cautioned her against revealing our identities to her employees at Sectate Manor. For practical purposes they were to be informed that, for a short period, two landscape engineers would be staying on the estate, commissioned in London by Miss Julia to survey the house and grounds with an eye toward bringing about whatever additions and improvements were deemed appropriate. As she informed us in Baker Street, her father had planned to instigate this very endeavor before taking ill, and so we hoped our presence should not prove conspicuous or peculiar.

Sectate Manor, as we approached in a dog-cart from the railway depot, was a sprawling Elizabethan house replete with turrets and moat, now dry, and almost completely obscured by a grove of oak and elm in the front, and sheltered by a quickly-rising hill to the rear. Although in late autumn the denuded trees allowed a partial view of the manse, one felt that in the full bloom of spring and summer one could easily miss seeing any of the house from the road. Despite its antiquity, the house and grounds appeared quite attractive and cheerful, and I found myself at a loss to imagine the sinister events of our client's narration. At last, our cart pulled up to the main entrance; Holmes paid the driver, and we stepped down upon the crushed stone drive and gazed upon our home for the unforeseeable future.

We were met at the main door by Ivers. He gave us a nod, a rather penetrating look, then motioned us inside with a curt gesture. Ivers was a burly, broad-shouldered bull of a man, short, but giving the appearance of having formidable strength. His face was wide and dark-browed, but with a small, mobile mouth and bright eyes. He wore dungarees, and had evidently been engaged in outdoor labor.

This man, then, led us to our rooms, where we left our cases and surveying equipment, which we had hastily leased in London. We freshened up and then were conducted to the massive dining room where we were greeted by a warm fire and the lady of the manor. After Ivers had left us, Holmes turned to me, out of earshot of Miss Sectate, and murmured, "I know this man, Watson, although I'd wager he doesn't know me. I have numerous clippings of his various activities in England, and have followed his career with some interest; we are dealing with Mr. Jack Sarine, one of Her Majesty's wilier subjects, and a deadly man to cross paths with. With Sarine in the mix, Miss Sectate is indeed in considerable jeopardy. Ah! But here is our hostess...."

After a cold dinner we adjourned with our client to the voluminous study. As we took a glass of sherry I noticed numerous periodicals and books dealing with the equestrian arts, and remarked idly on these to our hostess.

"Oh, yes," she replied. "I have a great interest in all things equine, dating back to my earliest childhood." A note of sadness entered her voice. "Scilla, my Arabian, was a championship mare. She was a gift from my father on my fourteenth birthday. I had intended to enter her in a show at Briarton next week, and was encouraged to think she could take top honors handily. But—well, that is over and done with forever."

Her voice trailed off and her young face had an expression upon it that made my heart go out to her.

Holmes put his glass of sherry down and arose. Taking me aside momentarily he said, *sotto voce*: "Watson, I fear we have an unpleasant chore to perform this evening." Holmes turned to Miss Sectate as he resumed, in normal tones: "I don't mean to appear insensitive, but I need to know a certain fact. Where are the remains of the departed Scilla buried? I must satisfy myself on one point."

Our client appeared startled for a brief moment, but then looked Holmes squarely in the eye as she replied, "Ivers buried her just east of the pond, by the giant oak there. This side of the stables. There is a small marker at the spot; I...I could not bear to let her be unceremoniously thrown in the earth!" And at this the girl covered her face with her hands and wept.

After an interval, Holmes spoke. "If you will supply us with a shovel

We were met at the main door by Ivers.

or two, and lead us to the site—I do not wish anyone else to know of our endeavor—we will do what must be done. Watson, if you will be so kind as to bring our lantern, and to escort the young lady back to the house after she has so obligingly shown us the grave, I think we may begin. There is something I must see for myself; or rather, not see."

With my friend's cryptic remark hanging in the air, we left the study. After gathering the necessary items, Miss Sectate conducted us, through a side egress and surreptitiously, from the manor and across an expanse of short-trimmed grass, until we had reached the ordained place. There was the marker, a little tablet of white-painted wood, inscribed thus: "Dear Scilla" and under: "Companion and Friend." Perhaps at no other time did the melancholy of our client's loneliness and isolation strike me so profoundly as then. I accompanied Miss Sectate back to the manor and soon rejoined Holmes at the horse's grave.

We spelled each other, then: digging, holding the lantern (shaded so as not to attract undue notice), then digging again, until we had uncovered the carcass of the slaughtered animal.

It was a grisly sight. Holmes knelt close with the lantern and examined the unfortunate creature for a minute, then hissed, "Cover it up!" We replaced the soil and marker and walked silently back to the house, a black silhouette against the light of the full moon behind it.

I looked at my companion as we entered the side entrance whence we had stole not long ago. His thin face was strained and white, and his eyes flashed with his rising anger. His voice grated as he spoke:

"This is cruelty incarnate, Watson. It comes near to turning my stomach."

Our much put-upon young lady was seated on a settee with the caretaker's wife when we entered the study again, having disposed of our equipment and cleaned up suitably. They were talking animatedly, but fell silent as we drew near. Mrs. Ivers, our client's newfound bosom friend, gazed up at Holmes and me, and as we returned her gaze I had to repress a start. The resemblance between the two women was remarkable! The large green eyes, auburn hair cut short, fair complexion; even the physical dimensions of the two were similar. The ladies might have been twins, so close was their likeness.

Miss Julia introduced us to her friend, careful to give our fabricated names and professions. Mrs. Ivers was polite, but I thought I detected a wary look in her otherwise frank gaze. Holmes, for his part, was all pleasantries and smiles, until announcing our intention to retire, and bade the ladies good night, as did I.

Once adjourned to our rooms, and after unpacking my own meager belongings, I took occasion to steal down the gaslit corridor to Sherlock Holmes' room. My friend opened his door to my soft tapping, and I entered to find Holmes loading and checking his revolver, and pacing rapidly about the small room. My curiosity concerning our endeavors of the evening, macabre as they were, had gotten the better of me, I confess, and even though I knew Holmes was loathe to talk about a case before it was completely clear to his marvelous brain, I begged him to clarify the puzzle to me.

Holmes abruptly ceased his pacing and looked intently at me. "Do you not see their plan, dear fellow? It is, alas, painfully obvious, which is not to take away an iota from the danger our client faces. We, too, Watson, may be in peril. I trust that does not dissuade you from seeing this little adventure through to its denouement?"

"Not a bit. You know I am with you every step of the way."

"Good old Watson! Tonight will see the climax of this little charade, in any event. Did you see the doctor?" I confessed I had not.

"Throughout our delightful supper, while you were so charmingly engaged in repartee with our hostess, I observed the physician scurrying about in the outer hall. Miss Sectate has informed me he stays in the room next to the father's chamber, on the third level."

"So as to avail himself to the father," I unnecessarily added.

"How can one avail oneself to a dead man? The father is deceased, and has been for some time, I daresay." Holmes added: "The doctor has seen to that. He is a crony of these two schemers, and the first on the scene in order to ensure that the father took ill; he is the poisoner of the original caretaker, Peters, and—along with Jack Sarine, our bogus 'Ivers'—a malevolent schemer of the first water. Do you see the theme yet?"

My head swam a little at these revelations. The father dead! Peters poisoned! Try as I might, I could not fathom the logical skein binding these crimes together, and confessed this to my friend.

"Ah, Watson, still not clear yet? Well, there will be time enough to paint a complete picture later. At this moment we have more urgent business to see to. Our client is in dire need of our intervention now, for unless I'm wrong, which is unlikely, tonight is the night her life is meant to be forfeit. Come along now, and pray bring your firearm…"

I followed Holmes down the dimly lit passageway and up a flight of stairs, until we were outside our client's door. We entered quietly, lit the candle on the bedside table, and waited. The clock over the fireplace in the room showed that one-half hour had elapsed before we heard a light step in the hallway, stopping outside the door. Miss Sectate entered the room, starting visibly as Holmes sprang toward her, finger at his lips urging her not to make a sound. He whispered in her ear for perhaps a minute, and by the feeble candle light I watched her expression go from dread to horror upon hearing his words.

Finally, Holmes bade the lady go into a small recess in a far corner of the room and crouch down, out of sight, and motioned me to secrete myself behind a large bureau. As he extinguished the candle and hid himself behind the headboard of the massive bed, he admonished me to keep my weapon at the ready.

"Now, Watson," he whispered, "we wait."

Two hours went by, marked by the chiming of the clock, but in that stygian darkness it seemed like ten. At last we heard muffled footsteps from the hall, and saw two points of ebon in the faint slit of light under the door.

Suddenly the door opened far enough to admit a black silhouette, as seen against the gaslight from the corridor, and closed again with nary a sound. We could barely hear the footsteps approaching the bed, when Holmes struck a match and in the same fluid motion lit the candle at bedside. By its light I saw the dull gleam of the revolver in my friend's hand, trained upon the figure whose aghast face now showed clearly in the flickering glow of the taper.

The intruder was a tall, gaunt man with bristling black beard, aquiline nose and small, stoat-like eyes. He wore a vest and black waist-coat, and in his right hand he held a hypodermic syringe. His left hand was stealing toward his pocket.

"I think it wise you not move that hand another inch," intoned Holmes gravely, "for two pistols are trained on you, and I assure you we will fire if you attempt to use either the syringe or the gun you are undoubtedly reaching for."

Holmes glanced at me. "Watson, let me introduce you to Dr. Hugo Nasser, late of the English Medical Society and preeminent among rogues still at large in the Kingdom. Dr. Nasser—excuse me, you no longer hold that professional title, do you?—Mr. Nasser, if you would humor us by placing your needle on the table to your right, and Watson, if you would relieve the gentleman of his pistol? Thank you."

Holmes smiled at our captive. "A pretty plan, and so near to fruition, too! Miss Julia Sectate could not have been more timely in her request for our aid. Another day would have seen her end. The constabulary of Kinson should be arriving soon, thanks to the telegram I sent earlier today from Baker Street. I think we would do well, Watson, to collect our sham physician's accomplices in this matter, as a courtesy to the police."

Our unwilling guest snarled at Holmes' reference to his apparent dismissal from the medical profession, but thereafter said nothing, even when our client came out from her hiding place to stare reproachfully at him.

We surprised "Ivers" and his wife in the kitchen, undoubtedly awaiting word from their co-conspirator that his nefarious task had been completed. When Holmes addressed Ivers as Jack Sarine, the latter knew his game was up and spat imprecations at us.

His wife merely glared at her exposed partners-in-crime and muttered, "I knew it wouldn't come off. I felt it!" She assiduously avoided meeting Miss Sectate's eyes, as if ashamed of her perfidy.

For Miss Julia's part, she only stared, with a curious mixture of horror and dumb-founded grief, at her former companion and friend; her look-alike had betrayed her so, although to what extent our client, and I, knew not at that time.

Holmes looked down at the three plotters, all sitting together at the kitchen table, and said lightly: "Come, come! Such glum looks. It was an ingenious plan, if a murderous one. No sympathy from me; I believe this young woman," indicating our client, "is more deserving of that emotion."

"I believe I hear our friends the law at the front door just now," Holmes said a moment later. "Watson, would you mind showing them in?" With a brief but sympathetic look at our client, Holmes murmured to her: "All this has, I know, been a great trial for you. But their plan has failed and you will, I am sure, soon gather the pieces of your life together. You are better off without such friends as these."

✗

We were back in our lodgings in Baker Street the following afternoon, idle and contemplative after the previous night's exploits. I was feigning interest in one of my medical texts while waiting for Sherlock Holmes, that so frequently unwilling raconteur, to enlighten me as to all that had transpired. I had been very patient, but my patience was near its end. At last I looked up and found him gazing at me with a sly smile and twinkling eyes.

"How goes the research, Watson?" he asked archly.

"Confound it, Holmes! You've been sitting there, puffing away on that damnable pipe of yours, waiting for me to break down and entreat your indulgence and explanation!" This was not unlike the man at all, I am sorry to say: The tale went untold until he was ready to tell it.

"Well, since you were so good to accompany me on our little excursion and lend your—as always—invaluable assistance, I suppose you are entitled to the full facts in the matter."

"One would hope so," I replied with slightly clenched teeth. "You have my full attention."

"You will recall, Watson, that, in our initial interview with the unfortunate Miss Sectate, she informed us of her virtual cloister within Sectate Manor throughout her youth, that she knew practically no one and no one knew her, save the servants and employees. That the father, John Sectate, dismissed these when he became depressed and ill: That fact rang an alarm with me immediately.

"Then there was the suspicious fact of Miss Sectate gradually being unable to visit with her father, supposedly due to the severe contagion of his sickness. I say 'supposedly' due to his illness being the work of our friend, Mr. Nasser, who insinuated himself into our little drama very early on, in order to set the stage for his confederates, Sarine and wife, masquerading as the Ivers.

"It was Nasser who sent the household staff packing, alleging to all it was the wish of John Sectate, he of official quarantine, which disallowed communication except through the good doctor, who no doubt bore occasional spurious messages from father to daughter, as he saw fit."

"Was he truly ill, Holmes?" I queried.

"I expect he was, for a while. He was being slowly poisoned with the same chemical later administered to the first caretaker, Peters, in a more lethal dosage. There is an extract from the venom of the Indian cobra which can produce the sort of seizures and behavior Miss Sectate attributed to Peters, and which in smaller amounts can produce hallucinations and psychosis. Perhaps the autopsy on the father will bear me out. As you know, I have studied and written extensively on the subject of rare poisons, and will wager a year's fees Nasser came across this one during his travels in India— oh, yes, Watson, the man is well known to me!"

"At any event," continued the great detective, "Nasser at some point allowed John Sectate to die. Perhaps 'allowed' is too weak a word in this instance. I suspected his demise when Miss Sectate told us that finally she was not able to see her father at all. I felt then that he was gone."

"As we found for certain last night," I said. "Without Sarine's wife's direction we might never have discovered his remains. That, at least, will go in her favor when her case is tried," I ventured.

Holmes blew smoke at the ceiling. "Do you remember the dying words of Peters, as related by Miss Sectate? 'Jim and I.' At the time I had no inkling of the meaning of it, 'Jim and I.' It was not until I gazed upon the face of 'Mrs. Ivers' that the true significance burst upon me: Peters was not saying 'Jim and I'; that was no reference to James Sectate, our client's unfortunate brother. Peters was saying 'Gemini'—Castor and Pollux, the Twins! Peters, the Astrology devotee, was as struck with the resemblance of the two ladies as we were, and in his delirium was making an oblique reference to one of his murderers, and I did not make the connection until I saw Sectate Manor's own 'twin.' I have no doubt Peters was held down by the Ivers in order to facilitate his rendezvous with Nasser's deadly little needle. With the symptoms similar to a heart attack, who would be the wiser? And with the good doctor's testament to heart failure on the death certificate—*fait accompli!*"

"Holmes," I asked, "what of the horse, Scilla? My guess is that Sarine killed the mare to quell any attempt by Miss Sectate to gain a measure of notice or renown by exhibiting her horse—a champion, allegedly—at any horse shows or competitions, as she was indeed intending to do."

"Excellent, Watson! You continually show promise! You are evidently catching on to the main premise: that any emergence on Miss Sectate's part from the anonymity of Sectate Manor would jeopardize the plan, which was to eliminate all who knew Miss Julia on sight. Servants, Peters, and John Sectate especially, must be removed in preparation to eventually eliminate Miss Julia—witness last night!—and replace her with a 'doppelgänger' who would claim the considerable inheritance when the father's death was announced to the world. I have no doubt our friend Nasser would have stage-managed that handily, causing neither undue comment nor suspicion."

Holmes went on: "The death of Peters had an added benefit in that "the Ivers'" could then enter and take over the vacant situation which was sure to be advertised in the papers. The pleasant addition of the wife as a companion to the lonely Miss Sectate virtually assured them the position.

Any suspicions or misgivings of our client pertaining to her father's illness or subsequent events, furthermore, could be lulled by her new friend's reassurance and cajoling, and communicated to Sarine and Nasser. Miss Sectate has been rather cruelly used, wouldn't you say, Watson?"

"To be sure, Holmes." I paused to think. "Another question, dear fellow. Why was it necessary to exhume the remains of the mare, when you already suspected Ivers, or rather, Sarine, had destroyed her?"

"I needed to be positive. If the horse had indeed been savaged by a pack of wild dogs or some wild animal, her corpus would have been at least partially consumed, or at very least mutilated to some extent. The signs would be there. They were not. The horse had been shot."

"Further," continued Sherlock Holmes, "there can be little doubt that Nasser and Sarine had planned this sequence of black deeds for some time. Witness the finding of Miss Sectate's 'double'; that took some little effort and time, I'm sure. Whether she truly is Sarine's wife I neither know nor care; that will come out in the assizes, fear not. It is, however, more than coincidence that she is so very close in appearance to our heiress."

One question continued to gnaw at me. "How in the name of all that's holy did you know that the blackguards would make their attempt on the young lady's life last night? They might have waited weeks or months!"

Holmes stood up and refilled his cherrywood from the slipper he had placed on the table next to his chair. "Three reasons, my dear fellow. First: this plot had been aboil for some time and they could not have disguised the fact of the father's murder much longer. Remember, Miss Sectate said her father was not expected to survive the week. As he went so must she, in order to bring in the ringer to lay claim to the inheritance."

"Second and third: our very selves, Watson! The fact of Miss Sectate leaving the manor for London, and returning with two strangers, landscapers, who were to stay for an undefined length of time must have driven home to our villains that she could not be contained within the house any longer and that, by contacting us, she was calling unwanted attention to herself."

"I wonder, Holmes, if you and I, in our spurious identities, faced a similar fate. As they were ready to murder Miss Sectate last night, might they not also feel it incumbent upon themselves to rid the manor, not to mention the world, of two bumbling landscape engineers who might note the remarkable resemblance between hostess and servant's wife, or who possibly would remain in the vicinity long enough to realize the substitution? At any rate, we had seen and dealt with the true mistress of the manor, something they did not welcome or, moreover—as evidenced by past fatalities—tolerate. I suppose we'll never know with any certainty...."

"Nor does it matter," rejoined the detective. "Speculation upon such nebulous and ultimately unprovable folderol is not only useless, but unhealthy to the logical faculties. However," he said with a quick smile, "I doubt I could have slept a night in that house with a clear expectation of awakening and greeting the new day."

"A singular case, Holmes! My hope is that our young lady will conquer her grief and past circumstances and go forth to greet the world. She has had heartbreak and loneliness enough. Perhaps she'll get hold of another champion Arabian, eh?"

"One would wish so, Watson. We should hope that she is the wiser and more worldly for her experiences of late. She will certainly be richer! And now, dear fellow, what do you say to an early dinner at Marco's? But first, perhaps, a little air of Sherzelle's...." And with that, he picked up his violin and began to play.

The End

WILLIAM RYDER THINNES discovered Sherlock through Howard Haycraft's *The Boy's Book of Great Detective Stories*, a paperback that he acquired in the early '60s. His father had the *The Complete Sherlock Holmes* (2 volume Doubleday edition), which he proceeded to read and reread, one story a night, through his sub-teens and teens. His all-time favorite is *The Hound of the Baskervilles*. He enjoys the Basil Rathbone and Jeremy Brett films. He is also a fan and collector of Raymond Chandler, and has a weakness for The Shadow and Doc Savage, pulp art in general, Blues and roots-oriented rock 'n roll, classic '30s and '40s [mainly] movies, *The Avengers* TV show and cartooning. He describes himself as "a fair artist," mainly in the areas of pencil portraits, caricature & cartooning. He is married with two children and the family dog, Asta.

Sherlock Holmes

in

"The Adventure of the Limehouse Werewolf"

By
Andrew Salmon

*M*y notes reveal that my return to Baker Street late on a dismal November night in the year 1896 marked the beginning of our investigation into the Limehouse Werewolf affair. I had not seen my friend, Sherlock Holmes, for a fortnight as I had been attending a wedding in Brighton. It had been a time of dreary inaction prior to my departure. The quiet had worn on Holmes and I feared the worse as he had gradually weaned himself off his particular habit. And so it was with a great deal of enthusiasm, and some trepidation, that I trod the familiar route to our lodgings.

It was not only with the intent of catching up with my companion that I eagerly anticipated our meeting. The Limehouse Werewolf was in all the papers, splashed across their front pages at that time. A man horribly mutilated—his identity withheld. One could not stop for a cigar or a drink without being bombarded by theories and speculations on the lips of everyone in the place: The Ripper was up to his old mischief. Springheel Jack was claiming his own. There seemed more theories than brains in the Empire and this alone must have incensed Holmes as nothing irritated him more than theories and conclusions in the absence of facts. When last I had seen Holmes, it had been just prior to the first murder. When word of it reached me, I almost cut my trip short and returned to London.

Given the lateness of the hour, I attempted a stealthy entrance but my efforts were in vain. Mrs. Hudson was awake in anticipation of my arrival. Holmes had awakened her to impart a message for my benefit before dashing out into the night an hour before. The purpose of the message was for me to join him in Limehouse the instant I arrived.

"Is it the werewolf?" I enquired of the venerable woman.

"Oh, I don't know, Dr. Watson," she replied, sleepily. "He tore off the moment I let in one of his ragged urchins."

Mrs. Hudson was referring to the Baker Street Irregulars—a group of wretched youths Holmes enlisted as his eyes and ears on the street.

The hour was late and there was some trouble finding a hansom after taking leave of Mrs. Hudson. However, find one I did, and I was soon rattling off towards the east end.

A considerable crowd had gathered at the murder scene. Casting my gaze into its teeming midst, I hunted my friend, but of Holmes there was no sign. This was hardly surprising as a half-dozen constables wrestled with the surging throng from an opium den nearby, which had been rousted in search of the killer. For murder it was. Lightning explosions of camera flash powder illuminated the scene and, as I fought my way through the dazed onlookers shuffling this way and that in zombie-like fashion, I caught sight of a sprawled figure face down in a small pool of blood turned black by the night. Reporters worked the crowd, hunting material for the morning editions. Yellow journalists stood calmly to one side, heads cocked. They would be creating their own tale out of whole cloth from whatever sensationalist details their mossy brains could conjure.

Still, I had not spied Holmes. The ferret face of Inspector Lestrade I saw several times as he moved about the scene with workmanlike efficiency. He had placed constables in a ring around the body. The photographers darted like cobras with their cameras between the men to capture grisly images. It had rained an hour before and the cobblestones glistened like so many stars around the gleaming full moon of a sewer grate between the surging crowd and the cordon of police. Finally Lestrade had had enough of the crowd's press and gave the order for the men surrounding the body to expand their protective circle and push the crowd back. The photographers had their plates and were the first to withdraw. The rest of the mob followed suit.

My toes were trod upon a half-dozen times during this retreat as I craned my neck in search of Sherlock Holmes. The curses I hurled at the clumsy clods fell on deaf ears. When the penumbra of onlookers was at its zenith, one of the constables strolling past the body suddenly yelped and fell to his knees beside the dead man.

"Gor, bless me!" wailed the constable half in fright, the other in wonder. "He's alive! He's alive!"

A murmur ran through the crowd which proceeded to push forward at once. Lestrade's head whipped around at the constable's exclamation and annoyance coloured his features while the constable pawed at the prostrate form futilely, unsure how to proceed. I employed my elbows to good advantage to work my way to the front of the crowd should my medical skills be needed.

"What's this, then?" demanded Lestrade who came to stand over his kneeling brethren.

"A groan! I heard—"

"Bleeding air trapped in the lungs!" chastised Lestrade as he glowered down at the policeman in his ill-fitting uniform. The man's helmet was sunk low on his brow, casting his features in shadow, but I could well imagine the conflicted anguish playing across his features. "An' you start a stampede with your rot? That man is dead!"

The berated constable ceased fumbling about the dead man and sat back on his haunches.

"Forgive me," he stammered. "I'm station night clark. That is... I don't often... cases...."

"Stop that!" roared Lestrade. "See to keeping that crowd back why don't you. Get away from the body!"

The constable rose unsteadily to his feet, nodded to Lestrade and then headed towards the sector of the crowd through which I had fought my way to the foremost rank. He stopped ten yards from me and stared. I saw his mouth drop open beneath the helmet's shadow across his upper lip.

"Inspector Lestrade!" he yelled in a high, keening voice. "Dr. Watson is here! I see 'im plain as day! He's bound to have that Sherlock Holmes with 'im! What should I do?"

The man's announcement turned the heads of the reporters in my direction. My recounting of our adventures had gained us some notoriety but our physical appearances were generally unknown, thus allowing us relative freedom of movement in our work. That idiot of a constable had singled me out and the reporters now converged. Lestrade was at the side of the stupid constable in an instant. Placing a hand in the center of the indiscreet police officer's back, he shoved the man forward.

"See to Dr. Watson's well-being," said he. "Damn fool!"

Eagerly, the constable threw himself into the crowd and, with the help of a few fellow officers, opened a clear path for me.

"Get him out of there!" shouted Lestrade over the heads of the crowd barely kept at bay.

Jostled and staggered, the constable stumbled up to me and seized me by the elbow.

"Come, Watson!" his voice hissed in my ear. "We must away."

It was my turn to gape. Standing before me was Holmes dressed as a policeman! I could not help but smile as I allowed myself to be guided out of the throng. Bloody cheek! Right under the nose of Lestrade! We reached the opposite side of the street as the coroner's wagon rattled up. For an instant all attention turned to the dead man about to be moved. A nearby alley presented itself. Holmes and I dashed up it.

Safely ensconced in Baker Street, Holmes removed his too-large policeman's greatcoat and helmet, a mischievous twinkle in his eyes. It had been a while since I'd last seen that in the sharp orbs of my friend and its return was welcome. I watched Holmes lay the coat across the top of an armchair and place the helmet on the mantle.

"You wouldn't rather tuck those out of sight?" asked I.

"Tosh! Lestrade may lack imagination, but his plodding tenacity is a matter of record," replied Holmes. "Even he will be able to solve the simple riddle of the vanishing constable. Until he arrives, we have much to discuss."

My eyes fell upon a quilted jacket of Chinese design, slippers and a black wig with pigtail and indicated them to Holmes. "I should say so. All Hallow's Eve was weeks back."

"The Oriental costume was for my forays into the opium trade, trying to drum up something to occupy my mind. I found nothing. Although I did hear rumours of a great Chinese mystic hiding somewhere in town. My attempts to meet with him came to nothing. This is hardly the matter at hand, Watson."

"This was another werewolf murder, then?"

"Undoubtedly. Although I reserve judgement on the species of the killer."

"You are not convinced the murderer turns into a wolf at the full moon?" I chided.

"Really, Watson," replied Holmes with disdain. "That is a discussion for another time. For the moment, my focus is on the victims."

"Whatever do you mean? The police have been tight-lipped from the outset."

"True. And what do you conclude from this?"

"Obviously they are withholding the name of the first victim from the press to keep the populace in the dark."

"Excellent, Watson. But why?"

Holmes took his chair by the fire and drew his knees up to his chest. Mrs. Hudson had possessed the foresight to build us a welcoming brazier in the hearth and the heat was much appreciated after the dank minutes by the water.

I gave this question some thought but could come to no conclusion. This I indicated to Holmes.

"Now the heart of it," continued Holmes. "The answer is simplicity itself. The murdered men were part of that sacred brotherhood of policemen. I suspected this after the first victim and confirmed my suspicions tonight."

"You masqueraded as a police constable so you could get close to the body, examine it."

"Precisely. As you know from exposure to London's finest, they are a close-knit lot and when one of their own goes down in the line of duty, they close ranks. This is why they have not yet sought me out—though that will change with Lestrade's arrival. They have kept the names out of the press to propagate the myth that they can keep the streets safe. If it got out that a maniac was killing policemen with impunity and could not be apprehended, chaos would ensue."

"What did you learn from the latest victim?"

"Much. First off, our victim was, at one time in his life, a seafaring man. A small tattoo on the skin between the thumb and forefinger of his left hand was a clear indication."

"The name of a ship?"

"No, a fan of four aces comprising as many suits above the word 'RUCKY.'"

"'RUCKY'? Was this the man's name, then, if not the name of a vessel?"

"I think not, although I have not ruled out either possibility."

"What else did your brief examination reveal?"

"His clothes were well-tailored though not expensive and the wear in the garments showed frequent use by their owner. In all, his garments were in keeping with what one would expect on a policeman's salary. His inspector's badge was in the left inside pocket of his coat. There lacked time to study it but we shall leave those details for Lestrade to impart. Squashed knuckles on either appendage told me he was not adverse to using his fists. Roughly thirty-five, I would say. Walked with a slight limp, right-handed—I could go on but the night wanes and Lestrade draws near."

"Nothing else of note? Only that he was a right-handed policeman?"

"There was one enigmatic item on the dead man's person. In itself it is a mere curiosity. However it becomes incongruous on the body of a savagely murdered police inspector. Ah, but there is Lestrade upon the stairs. Let us welcome him."

Any further revelations did, indeed, have to wait as Mrs. Hudson, clearly hampered by the lateness of the hour, showed Inspector Lestrade into our rooms. The inspector was in an agitated state and bowled past the woman, almost toppling her to the floor.

"What do you think you're playing at?" railed Lestrade at Holmes. "Impersonating a policeman? I could have you in irons for that!"

Holmes cared not a whit for this tirade. He lurched out of his chair and proceeded to the side of Mrs. Hudson to ascertain that she'd not be injured in any way by Lestrade's oafish behaviour.

"Have a care, Inspector!" cautioned Holmes.

This seemed to cool Lestrade's hot temper somewhat. Sheepishly he nodded his apologies to Mrs. Hudson who accepted them before quitting the room. Clutching at the brim of his hat, his clothes dripping with the icy rain that had begun, Lestrade shuffled from one foot to the next as Holmes resumed his seat by the fire.

"Well, come and warm yourself then," offered Holmes.

Lestrade grimaced at the sight of the policeman's uniform draped about the place, then stepped up to the hearth and extended his hands. The gaze of my friend turned to Lestrade and those hard eyes fixed on the man's tense back. For a moment, those eyes softened and the caring heart of Holmes lit them from within.

"Come, Lestrade," said he. "You are among friends."

"You, sirs, are no friends of mine." Lestrade kept his head down, his gaze riveted on the dancing flames.

I knew, as did Holmes, that Lestrade spoke from tension. After all, upon hearing my presence revealed to the crowd, his first thought was for my safety. He did not see through Holmes' disguise and damned himself for it as he damned his inability to apprehend this so-called werewolf who had now struck twice and fled without a trace. Holmes selected a singular approach for bringing Lestrade out of his brown study.

"My efforts tonight were but an act of desperation on my part," said he. "A diabolical murderer roams the streets and you, Inspector, are honour bound to leave no stone unturned, to utilize every resource to catch him. My not insignificant talents are a proven resource and I place them at your disposal as I have done in the past. Do not let pride or a laudable, though misguided, sense of loyalty shut me out. Not when there are lives at risk. Come, Lestrade."

After a seemingly unending silence, Lestrade's shoulders slumped perceptibly and a sigh passed his lips.

"What don't you know?" asked he at last, his voice but a whisper.

This turn of events invigorated Holmes, who clapped Lestrade on the shoulder then resumed his seat. Eyes dancing in the firelight, Holmes filled his pipe and puffed contemplatively for a moment or two.

"The first victim," said he. "A police inspector?"

"He was."

"Same tattoo on the left hand?"

Lestrade nodded.

"How far did you get with that?"

"It's of no consequence," said Lestrade. "They were merchantmen years ago. Collar the first ten seamen you find down Portsmouth way and you'll find as many tattoos."

"However we cannot exclude the possibility that the men knew each other before joining the force."

"I suppose so. Both had been on the force ten years. Quite a bit of time for their past lives to bear on their deaths. We have been hunting witnesses, running to ground anyone they might have come in contact with under the pretext of duty. Informants and the like."

"Hold a moment, if you please," said Holmes. "Names of the victims?"

"Perry Waters and Wilbur Morse. We just returned from the Morse killing."

"Ah, thank you. Waters and Morse. Go on."

"There's not much else at the moment. An inspector has more eyes and ears on the street than fingers and those connections have connections as numerous as the stars in Heaven. We'll be a while tracking them all down."

"You proceed on the assumption the murderer knew his victims."

"Tops the notion of a random killer arbitrarily slaughtering two police-men in succession."

Holmes nodded his agreement.

"Was a valuable Chinese fashion accessory found on the body of Waters as well?"

"What is this?" asked I.

By this time Lestrade had removed his greatcoat and had hauled a wooden chair close to the fire. However, he only perched on it for a moment. He was up and pacing, running his hands through his hair.

"Forgive me, Watson," replied Holmes. "I was about to explain this when the good inspector arrived. In the breast pocket of Morse's coat was a Chinese fan. Very ornate, very old. I'd say Song Dynasty by the tips protruding from the pocket. I found it of singular interest due to its rather substantial value."

"I'm certain the fan is but a trifle. Stock and trade in any port of call on God's green earth," said Lestrade. "A bauble for a lady friend in exchange for services rendered. Such things are not uncommon. As to your question, no, Waters had nothing like that on him when his body was discovered."

"Waters was attacked in the vicinity of a clinic, if memory serves," said Holmes.

"That is correct."

"And the constables who found him hurried him there in hope of saving his life."

"Some hope. They panicked for one of their own. No matter in the end."

"Yes, because neither Waters or Morse were murdered where their bodies were found."

"Exactly."

Here Holmes requested the addresses for the two dead men. Lestrade read them out off a notepad and Holmes and I committed them to memory.

"Both men were on duty when they were killed?" asked Holmes.

"No. Waters and Morse worked the daylight shift."

"That may be significant. Only the Wapping address of Waters could be said to be anywhere near the Limehouse docks, and both men were off duty. So why were they there?"

"A police investigator is never truly off duty," replied Lestrade. "There is always an angle to follow up. You know that as well as I."

"True, true."

"Well, what do you make of it?" asked Lestrade.

Holmes tapped out the remains of his pipe.

"Any conclusions hastily drawn are more guesswork than anything else at this point. You have provided a start for our investigation, nothing more."

"As to that," said Lestrade. "I advise discretion. The lads are stirred up by this one. The murder of police officers is a personal affront to any lawman. They won't take kindly to civilians sticking their noses into police business and they won't be reticent in letting you know how they feel."

"We will tread softly," said Holmes. "I give you my word on that. Watson?"

I replied likewise.

We bade Lestrade good night despite the deep bags under the man's beady eyes. He accepted our wishes though he knew better than we did that it would not be a good night. It lacked only a few hours until daylight and perhaps that was a blessing for Inspector Lestrade. For Holmes and myself it was a time to rest up for the task ahead.

Morning found us somewhat bleary-eyed but no less committed to the task before us. To my surprise our first stop was not to be the home of Wilbur Morse or even the station house to make discreet enquiries or learn what progress Lestrade might have made in his investigation. Instead Holmes bounded out to the waiting hansom, flinging the Wapping address of Perry Waters at the driver before I had settled into my seat.

Inspector Waters had leased rooms above a bakery, and the odour wafting over us as we stepped down twenty minutes later in front of the place was intoxicating. The landlord—a surly, scruffy, short man—took

"Well, what do you make of it?" asked Lestrade.

our arrival as an invitation to rail against the world in general and the police in particular since Scotland Yard had not cleared him to let out the rooms, which had been unoccupied since the murder of the tenant two weeks ago. Nothing official, of course, but a fading yellow bruise upon the man's unshaven left cheek bespoke a particular form of negotiation. We gleaned from the man his name was Clark, that he owned the entire flat, including the bakery. We were granted ten minutes to examine the rooms. For a fee.

The state of the flat was my second surprise that morning. I had expected a bachelor's habitual squalor. Without question Perry Waters lived very well on a policeman's salary. The rooms were not sumptuous by any stretch of the imagination. However, the working class look to the place was, undoubtedly, a careful affectation.

"Is it any wonder that Waters' friends on the force are keeping the curious out of here?" asked Holmes rhetorically. He trod across the carpet to a cupboard and pulled open a drawer. "That rug is Persian. Ah, and here we have silver. A full set as well. That painting behind you, Watson, in the horrid, green frame is an E.C. Williams landscape. If that isn't a goose down comforter on the four-poster in the bedroom, I'll eat it."

The bedroom was just visible through the open door leading off from the parlour and Holmes directed his steps there. I cast my gaze about while he banged drawers around out of sight. Even to my untrained eye, the quality of the furnishings could not be disputed. Yes, Waters was doing very well before he was killed. I joined Holmes in the bedroom.

A sea chest before the sprawling bed caught my eye. Holmes had not as yet examined it. His murmurs reached me from the closet he was scrutinizing. I removed a mound of folded blankets from atop the chest, which was locked. I saw to that obstacle with a nearby letter opener and raised the lid.

"No sign of it," said Holmes cryptically as he emerged from the closet. "Good, Watson, you have anticipated me. The chest is next."

Kneeling, he joined me in inspecting the contents.

"We've confirmed that Waters was a seaman at least," I observed.

"Indeed. However, we shall get to any past connections in due time."

Holmes did not linger over the meagre contents of the chest: A few cardigans, some coins of foreign currency, a rattle which Holmes deemed Polynesian and a small, black ornamental box caked with clumped snuff. A large bundle of bank notes drew our attention. Although of interest to our investigation, it did not overtly convict the dead man.

Holmes stood in the middle of the room, his gaze gliding over its walls and furnishings as he hunted some place of concealment he might have overlooked.

"I suspect they've stolen it," said he at last.

"Whatever do you mean? It's unlikely a thief would risk tampering with a place under police watch."

"Oh, it was never here. I needed to confirm that. Yes, they've pinched it. I'm certain of it. Come, Watson!"

There was no finding a cab where we were and walking was our only alternative. The clinic was in Limehouse though set back from the river.

It was still early and there remained some hope of catching the night shift as they wound up their nocturnal hours. From the admitting clerk Holmes obtained the names of the two men who had assisted the police when Waters had been rushed inside. We also learned that Ian Howard and Bill Wylie were on the previous night's schedule.

"Up for some theatre, Watson?" asked Holmes as we made our way to the staff lockers.

"I do not even know why we are here."

"You've not hit on it, then? We must take on the identity of police once again with this rabble. I think you'll make an excellent brute."

"I don't know how to take that."

Holmes continued, oblivious to my remark. "Remain silent with Howard and Wylie. They shall create the threat in their minds and do our work for us."

Mystified I followed Holmes along the brick archway to the changing rooms. Men moved about in various states of undress and the lights overhead contrasted with the gloom of the passageway.

"Howard and Wylie," demanded Holmes, injecting lawful authority into his tone. The man he addressed cocked a thumb to the right. Two men at the end of the aisle were stuffing hospital whites into small duffles, cigarettes dangling from their lower lips.

"Wylie, Howard," said Holmes with his best police sneer. "We worked with Perry Waters. Get me? No beating around the bush, you two. Where is it? Come, now! We've not got all day."

The men exchanged guilty looks only amateurs can muster, then adopted a hard line of their own.

"Piss off!" said Howard. "We'll not answer to you."

"You'll say it or we'll bleed it out of you," countered Holmes. "We know you nicked it. Now, for the last time, where is it?"

I did my best at this point to look imposing and this had the desired effect on Wylie. He paled and licked his lips nervously.

"H-He was dead, what's the 'arm?"

"Shut it!" cautioned Howard.

"None of that!" Holmes shook his fist under the nose of Wylie. "Out with it!"

Wylie's gaze darted but then he gave up and we got the story out of him.

The night Perry Waters died had been a quiet one until the two constables had burst through the admittance door. Waters was held between them, the body oozing blood from the slashes inflicted upon the man. It had fallen to the two orderlies to strip the body for the doctor's inspection and while engaged in this, they had come across a certain item of value. When pressed, they admitted taking a brooch from the breast pocket of the corpse and gave the justification that the doctor would have stolen it should they have refrained from doing so.

"Where is it, then?" demanded Holmes when their halting litany of sins had ended.

"We took it to the Jew," replied Howard, sulkily. "Next street but one."

"Describe the brooch."

"A—A green bird and a bunch of flowers," stammered Wylie. "In the water like."

With a stiff warning from Holmes to keep to the straight and narrow, we left the two confounded thieves and found ourselves on the street once more.

"What say you we obtain the brooch, then have our luncheon?" asked Holmes.

It was early yet but my stomach, encouraged by the bakery earlier, was not opposed to the notion and I agreed heartily.

The pawnbroker gave us no trouble. Unaware of the item's value given its source as well as our feigned indifference in acquiring it, the man still drove what he perceived as a hard bargain and we exited with the item.

"I make the connection that both of these items are Chinese in origin," said I. "But I fail to see their deeper significance with regards to the murders."

The eyes of Holmes gleamed.

"Yes, the Asian ancestry is of some importance, but for the moment, it is the value of the pieces that strikes my interest."

"How so? Lestrade is convinced they are but trifles the men distributed for the favours of fallen women."

"He is incorrect in his assumption."

"Then why did the men carry them?"

"Ah, there is the answer. I am convinced they did not."

"I have lost the scent."

"Value, Watson. Take the fan. Song Dynasty was my assessment and I stand by that. A fan of this vintage, in the exceptional condition of the one in question is not something one finds on a street corner or even in the finest antique shops on Bond Street. The fan is priceless and more suited to a museum than the marketplace."

"And the brooch?"

Holmes whipped the item out of his pocket and handed it to me.

"Jade with solid silver inlay. Feel the weight of it. I put it, at a guess, mid-Jin Dynasty."

"And, like the fan, too valuable for even policemen with sticky fingers to manage."

"You have it, Watson."

"Then how did they come to have them on their person at the time of death?"

"To answer that conclusively I shall need to see the fan."

"Lestrade."

"Indeed. But first let us refresh ourselves."

The victuals were precisely what the doctor ordered. Holmes had refused to discuss the case as we dined and was still in a lather from his discourse on the role of pewter in the fall of Rome when we returned to the streets. That topic had been of some general interest to a medical man such as myself but the Limehouse Werewolf knocked any thought along historical lines out of my head. It was my fervent hope that Lestrade could shed some light on the mystery. A crazed lunatic was ripping policemen to tatters and we were chasing priceless Chinese artifacts. I could make no sense of it. We sent a runner into the Yard with a note for Lestrade. Holmes had taken pains to render a note that was sufficiently cryptic so as to prevent station gossip while at the same time not taxing upon the deductive powers of the inspector.

We returned to Baker Street where Holmes immediately set about continuing the experiments on oxidation which had partly occupied his thoughts until the second murder. Having learned my lesson at lunch, I did not press him for any thoughts or conclusions on the case. Instead, I tried *Marcus Aurelius* but the volume could not hold my attention in light of our current pursuit and I was left mulling over what little we knew while keeping one eye on the clock for Lestrade.

When the Inspector finally arrived, I leapt out of my seat to show him in. Holmes did not demonstrate that he was even aware Lestrade has entered the room. He studied the retort bubbling above a small flame for a moment or two, then he extinguished the burner and swung his tall frame around, withdrawing the brooch from a coat pocket at the same time.

"From the body of Perry Waters. Another valuable antique of Chinese origin."

Lestrade took the brooch and looked it over as Holmes explained how we came by the bauble. The inspector laughed in his throat.

"This is what you have been wasting your time with? I told you these are but coin of the realm."

"Not so," said Holmes simply. "The value of these items cannot be disputed. They did not belong to Waters nor Morse."

"They were found on the bodies," said Lestrade.

"True. But they did not belong to the victims. Of this I am certain."

"Then how in blazes did they get there?"

"Your contention is that the murderer placed them on the bodies," said I.

"Nonsense!"

"Watson has it, Lestrade," said Holmes. "I shall reason it out for you. The items are rare antiquities. Their value cannot be estimated. Whatever their worth, they are beyond the means of Inspectors Waters and Morse. The scarcity of the items render it all but impossible that the two murdered men stumbled upon them by pure chance. Observe the condition of the items."

Lestrade removed the fan from his inside coat pocket and gingerly opened it. The fan was in immaculate shape despite its delicacy and age.

"As I suspected, Song Dynasty and in near flawless condition. Does that look as if it has knocked about in thrift shops for a century or two? Clearly not. Very well. If the two men did not own these items and could not obtain them easily let alone have the means to purchase them, then how did they get into their pockets after they were dead? The answer is obvious: the murderer placed them there."

"But why?" asked I.

"Who knows?" replied Lestrade. "The man is a lunatic."

"That has not been proven," said Holmes. "What can we deduce about the murderer? This individual is intelligent—at least in the diabolical sense. He or she is wealthy or has an associate who is very well off. Both items found on the bodies are Chinese in origin which suggests, but does not confirm, that our murderer is, in fact, Chinese. We have made some headway here but must bridge some gaps in our reasoning."

"I may be of assistance in that regard," said Lestrade. "We've been looking into the background of the two dead men. Waters and Morse were both merchantmen and knocked about in their youths. We've got the names of three ships they sailed on."

"We need only concern ourselves with the last of those three."

"Why do you say that?"

"Because at the end of that last voyage, they gave up the life of a seaman. Why?"

"I can't answer that," said Lestrade. "But I can tell you that the first ship on the list went down in a storm six years ago. The second is seeing service in Canada after having changed hands."

"The third?"

"*Banshee* by name. Captain Herbert Lewis. She is a channel runner at present. In her day, she got around a bit more freely."

"If the Orient was one of her previous destinations, we may have another avenue of investigation."

"We won't know until she gets back tomorrow. She's off the French coast at the moment. I've sent a telegraph message through an exporting concern asking only after her return date. If she gets wind of police interest and her captain is up to something illicit, we might scare her off."

"Good thinking Lestrade," said Holmes. "For the moment, it is imperative that we…."

The shrill blast of a police whistle cut Holmes off in his observations. Lestrade bolted to the door. Anxious moments passed while we waited for the inspector's return. Muffled voices raised in alarm reached us through the closed windows and above the crackling of the fire.

Lestrade thrust his head through the open door. "The bugger has struck again! Come on!"

For the sake of appearances, we did not travel with Lestrade and his trustworthy minions. Instead we learned the location of the third victim, Regent's Canal, and proceeded there in a separate hansom by an alternate route. When we approached our destination, I instructed the driver to take Narrow Street after Lestrade's wagon went north on Medland.

Alighting from the cab, we followed the gathering crowd to the mouth of an alley a stone's throw from the turbid water of the canal. Knowing the sensitivity of the police with regards to our involvement in the case,

Holmes skirted the outer fringe of the crowd where we successfully concealed our presence while remaining within earshot of Lestrade. Of the body we could see nothing through the intervening cordon of the crowd and police. To his credit, Lestrade guessed our play though he could not see us and pitched his voice accordingly when the morgue wagon arrived. Calling across to the driver when he could have as easily approached the vehicle, Lestrade gave us our instructions via his address to the driver.

"Salmon Lane is your best bet, driver!" said he in a half-shout. "Go by way of the canal. We have cleared a path."

I felt the insistent hand of Holmes on my elbow and we hastily withdrew to the water's edge.

"Our good friend, Lestrade, has shown us the way," said Holmes. "The causeway is our destination and we must make haste if we are to outdistance the wagon. I do wish we'd had the foresight to bring opera glasses along. Well, we are not all-knowing, are we? We shall make do, I suppose."

I did not immediately comprehend what Holmes meant by all this, but it all made sense once we reached the causeway. The short, brick span carried pedestrians over the road to the nearby railway line, providing a bird's eye view not only of the canal but also over the rooftops of the neighbourhood. Holmes and I loitered about under the guise of enjoying a cigarette for a moment or two as we waited for the wagon to pass under the bridge.

The wagon clattered around the corner behind us with its police escort. The force had lost another brother and those who could be spared from the crime scene tagged along out of respect. Lestrade puffed a cigar from the rear bed next to the shrouded corpse, the flare bathing his features in ochre relief. Following my friend's gaze under the bridge, I perceived a slight curve beneath the railway superstructure. The wagon would have to slow down to navigate the turn, which had been rendered further impassable by the unfinished job a work crew had been performing on the brickwork. This brief halt would provide the best chance at getting a look at the corpse.

The wagon now rattled by at our backs and we shielded our features. Given the hour, the causeway was normally unpopulated and our presence would have been conspicuous, but word of the murder had spread and the curious now joined us on the span. The wagon paused a moment to bump over the trolley tracks and all I could see was the flare of Lestrade's cigar as the wagon was bathed in shadow.

Sure enough it came to a full stop at the bend while the horses tested their footing on the uncertain stones. Lestrade crouched and, hidden from view on the ground by the high walls of the wagon, he drew back the blanket covering the corpse while in the act of adjusting it. At one point, Lestrade held up a white object. He did this quickly though the driver's back was to him and the man seemed focused on the horses. The wagon jerked as the horses made up their minds to navigate the curb and soon the conveyance and its police escort dwindled from my sight.

"The werewolf. Without question."

"If by that do you mean are we dealing with the same murderer? The answer is yes. The body had been savaged in a manner consistent with the other victims."

We started down the way we came.

"What was it Lestrade held up?"

"An ornate, ivory, decorative hair comb."

"Of Chinese origin?"

"And of antique vintage. The comb leaves no room for doubt," said he. "Now we can begin to delve into the heart of these murders. Let us return to where the body was discovered. We may learn a thing or two more before Lestrade seeks us out with the victim's name."

His features clouded with frustration as we left the canal behind.

"The case was slow revealing itself to me and now another police officer is dead. I should have been quicker in putting it together. I shall seek to increase the rapidity of my deductions forthwith lest innocent lives be lost."

"Do not recriminate yourself," said I. "One cannot predict lunacy."

"Rot! This is no madman, Watson! This is no feral, hairy beast! Does a lunatic murder three police officers, plant priceless relics on them and then display the corpses in the street with nary a witness?"

Hot with his perceived failings, Holmes stalked off towards the slowly dispersing crowd and I had to hasten my steps to catch him. The crowd had thinned noticeably by the time we returned to where the body had been discovered. A few knots of men remained, their heads close together as they discussed this latest act of the Limehouse Werewolf. The police were gone as well—either back to their duties or accompanying the slain to the morgue as part of the respectful procession we had just left.

Holmes went to the section of cobblestones where the body had lain. As with the other murders, there was little or no blood save that which had oozed from the lifeless body before it had been found. Holmes was deep in thought, tormented by self-imposed anguish and I thought it best to let my friend work through his thoughts without making an attempt to intervene. My heel rang on a manhole cover as I turned away. Holmes gave no reaction to the sudden noise. If he was even aware of my departure, he gave no sign.

A flurry of motion drew my attention to one cluster of gentlemen. They were all talking at once and shuffled about as though a tiger had suddenly been dropped in their midst. Joining the group, I instantly saw the subject of their excitement. The man that stood among them was the neighbourhood lamplighter. He was a short mouse of a man with a bulbous nose and generous lips. His bleary eyes danced with the memory of something he wished to relate.

"I sawr the beast, I did!" he blurted past toothless gums. "Plain as I'm standing here!"

"You did not tell the police?" asked I.

"Not going to loiter about, me. I'se sure to lose me situation if I stopped to jabber when I'se should be doin' me route. Well, I'se done it now and heres I am! It's a wonder I could hold the pole steady arfter what I clapped eyes on."

"What did you see?" asked Holmes, suddenly by my side.

"'Orrible! 'Orrible! Shaggy as a dog with eyes glowin' red. Only on two legs! A man!"

"The werewolf!" a member of the crowd announced.

"Aye, it was! An he's no creation the good Lord ever placed on this earth."

"Spare the dramatics and speak plain, man," demanded Holmes. "Tell us what you saw and there's money in it for you."

This had the desired effect and some of the fire in the man dimmed to cold greed. Coins clinked as they changed hands and he told us what he knew. The man, Leonard Smythe was his name, had begun his duties at dusk with nothing out of the ordinary occurring. However, upon rounding the corner of Medland Street and London Street, he spied a hairy figure crouched menacingly over the prostrate form of the dead policeman.

"Dressed like a right gentlemen, he was! As God is my witness."

The newspapers had provided lurid depictions of a hairy monster on their front pages and these fictional images spurred questions as to the appearance of the creature.

"Naw," Smythe said, shaking his head. "Its clothes waren't torn. Only its shoes were mucked about. Looked like he was a-comin' from the theatre or some such like."

"What did this creature do?" asked Holmes.

"It leaned over the dead man, rippin' his throat out, I'll wager, though I couldn't see for sure as the killing took place in the black shadows. Then it spranged away like the very hound of hell. Only it must have caught me scent because it whirled around and looked back at me with them eyes of Hell. I was sunk in shadow by this time. If it had a-seen me, me blood would be runnin' in the street. Of that I'se sure!"

"Was this creature tall or short?"

"Short, like a animal. Like a dog."

"Yet you claim it stood on two legs and wore a suit of clothes," added Holmes.

"It did stand on two legs and wore clothes. It's face was wooly as a bear! I won't be called a liar!"

These revelations touched off a flurry of speculation which attributed to the werewolf all manner of deviltry. Holmes, ignoring Smythe's indignation, had no interest in what followed and we withdrew from the crowd. Our steps took us to Narrow Street in the direction of the Limehouse Pier. Holmes appeared to be in good spirits even though Smythe's claims had, apparently, contradicted my friend's claim that we were not looking for a monster. I put this question to him.

"Explanations can wait for the present," replied Holmes. "We have much ground to cover in very little time. Also, from Lestrade we will need the name of this latest victim. We are close to our quarry, Watson, but we shall have to work hard to close the gap."

I trusted my friend's conclusions, though I could not share in his enthusiasm. He had just seen his assertion that we were not after a monster repudiated and yet took this setback as a leap forward.

"Let us home, Watson," said Holmes. "Rest for the day ahead, eh? Also we must have Lestrade's official input if we are to bring this matter to a satisfactory conclusion."

Lestrade breakfasted with us the next morning. Holmes abstained as was his wont while on a case. Mrs. Hudson had been informed by Holmes that the good inspector would be joining us, and the woman had outdone herself. Over coffee, Holmes turned his piercing gaze to Lestrade and awaited the information the man had brought to the table. At this point there was no need for preamble and Lestrade got right to it.

"The murdered man was James Carter. A police inspector like the other victims. His wounds match those on the other victims, and he was not killed where he was found. There is no doubt his murder is connected."

"So I surmised," said Holmes. "I was too far away to be certain when I viewed the body. Did Inspector Carter have the same tattoo as the others?"

Lestrade nodded.

"Ah."

"Have you uncovered any other connection between the dead men?" asked I.

"Not at present," replied Lestrade, dabbing at his lips. "The *Banshee* docks today. Whether I can make it down to see Captain Lewis is another matter."

"I take it Mr. Smythe presented himself at headquarters," said Holmes.

"He did. Looks like he made the rounds of every paper in town as well. All of London is out for the werewolf's blood," complained Lestrade. "It was bad before but nothing like this. We've got crackpots seeing hairy beasts in every teapot and around every corner. The usual soft heads are confessing that they are the werewolf, the devil's spawn. It is pandemonium at headquarters and the Commissioner wants the cases closed. The men have done a sweep, turned up a score of mentally unbalanced suspects. And all must be investigated as a matter of course. One never knows.... You can meet them. I can arrange it. It will have to be in the wee hours, though."

"That won't be necessary," said Holmes. "Perhaps we can lighten your burden somewhat. It is in all of our best interests that Captain Lewis provides the background we need on the victims and so I propose that Watson and I meet with the man."

"I appreciate the offer," said Lestrade. "But this is a police matter."

Holmes held up a restraining hand. "Allow me to finish. I do not wish to disparage merchantmen as a class, but everyone here knows that most are not above slipping a little illicit business in with the honest. Lestrade, for all of your general affability, every inch of you screams policeman. This Captain Lewis will take one look at you and close up like an oyster. On the other hand, Watson and I can present ourselves to the man and may get more out of him in the process. Clearly you can see the sense in such an approach."

Lestrade was silent for a moment as his burning desire to bring the murderer to heel battled with the logic of Holmes' assessment of the situation.

"There's merit in what you say," he admitted at last. "All right. Do it your way and let me know what you find out."

"Excellent. In what name did you send the telegram?"

"Smith."

"Original."

"Best I could come up with on short notice and little sleep. Damn this case!"

With that, Lestrade pushed away from the table. He thanked us for our hospitality and, with a slightly resigned air, left to take up his duty to the city.

The London docks were much altered by daylight. What before was shrouded in eerie silence and shadow fairly thrummed with activity as Holmes and I alighted from our cab. Water birds circled in the crisp blue sky and their calls were added to the cacophonous back and forth bellows between stevedores and ships' officers as wooden timbers creaked and groaned. Bells clanged. Feet pounded. Masts like a drifting forest, the breeze sang in the rigging where men clambered up and down like monkeys. And everywhere was motion. We had arrived ahead of *Banshee* but she was expected presently.

At last the *Banshee* appeared before us, putting an end to our wait. She was a two-masted, down at heel schooner sagging in the water. Holmes had been quiet all the while and, as to what went on in his mind, I have no clue. I had learned from him not to leap to conclusions without facts yet it was my fervent hope that Captain Lewis would be able to suggest a connection between the murdered men which would shed light on the affair before another man was killed or the murderer fled.

"We will have our chance at this werewolf," said Holmes, as if reading my mind. "Captain Lewis and the *Banshee* will show us the way. I am certain of it, which is why I convinced Lestrade to permit us to question the man."

"Holmes! Surely you are not thinking we need to best Lestrade at a time like this."

"Nothing of the sort. You misconstrue my motivation. Enough. The *Banshee* is secure. Come, let us board."

The deck of the vessel buzzed with activity. Lines were made fast and a ramp was provided for us to board. We were not present in any official capacity and therefore lost ourselves in the array of colourful businessmen with legitimate concerns for the vessel and her cargo and thus boarded undetected. Captain Lewis emerged from his cabin to greet his assembled visitors.

He was of average height and build, fastidious about his appearance since he looked as if he'd just stepped from a board room and not freshly returned from a sea voyage. Short, dark hair, hatless with large brown eyes

We had arrived ahead of Banshee *but she was expected presently.*

and a thin nose, his cruel lips twisted as he adopted a welcoming manner. The group moved inside and Holmes and I were content to wait as the captain saw to various bills of lading and signed orders for the removal of cargo while two bruisers stood watch just inside the door. Then it was our turn. Lewis turned his frank, unwavering gaze towards us and his thick eyebrows rose a fraction in expectation.

"The name is Smith," lied Holmes, shaking the man's hand as the last of the businessmen filed out. "Leland Smith. And this is my confidential associate, Mr. Perkins. I cabled you on a matter of business a day or so ago."

"Yes," Lewis said, his gaze appraising. "You enquired as to when *Banshee* would make London."

"Quite so."

"What is your interest in my ship?"

This was the crux of the matter. Holmes proceeded smoothly, unfazed by the import behind his next words, and I was acutely aware of the guards behind us. He made a show of dropping all pretence. A remarkable transformation took place as Holmes twisted his features and form into that of a shrewd, nervous criminal.

"You know they got Waters," said he, his voice dipping conspiratorially. "What you don't know is that they got Morse and Carter these last two days."

Lewis stiffened and his gaze shifted. "I do not know the men you are referring to."

"Come, now!" said Holmes, indignant. "There's no time for that. We are three down. Neither you nor I want to be the fourth."

Lewis paused, sizing Holmes up. For his part, Holmes' flawless portrayal had me convinced we lived a life of crime. He met the gaze of Lewis. From his stance to the tone of his voice, no detail had been overlooked and the performance worked on Lewis as well.

"Morse and Carter have connections on the force," said the captain with reluctance.

Holmes smiled but there was no humour in it. "There! You have just admitted complicity in a smuggling operation and the evidence is still aboard this ship. Have I or my associate put police whistles to our lips? Do you hear police boots on the gangway?"

Only the sound of normal routine reached our ears.

"If you are satisfied, let us work on our mutual problem together for we have little time. If not, let us draw pistols and bathe in blood. As you are the captain of this ship, our final course is up to you. What will it be?"

Lewis' gaze turned inward as he considered the angles. "Morse and Carter won't talk."

"Agreed. They are both dead."

Lewis had not been expecting that. He paled. "Who?"

"Half the police force are chasing a werewolf, the other are digging into connections between the dead men? How long before they hit on *Banshee*?"

"Aye, it's there for the finding. Can't say I know what good it will do them."

"You don't, eh? What if the police become convinced this ship is the sole connection between the men. They'll storm aboard like rats. Then where will we be?"

"What's all this rot about a werewolf?"

"Waters and Morse were savaged," explained Holmes. "The papers put this down to a bloodthirsty beast roaming the streets."

Seamen being superstitious by nature, the news did not sit well with Lewis, though he attempted to wave the information away. He grunted, his mind made up.

"The cargo has cost me too much already. I'll not dump it to jump at shadows. Tell the Giant we will offload tonight."

"Every hour is precious ..." began Holmes.

"The Giant has his end buttoned down. I will do nothing to cross him. He'll get us through all right."

"As you say. Is there any evidence linking the dead men to this ship? Besides the tattoos and the registry logs?"

Lewis shook his head. "Those damned tattoos. I told the conceited fools they might as well hang signs around their necks."

"There's been no mention of them in the papers so far, but the police would be blind to have missed them, even if they don't know what the playing cards mean."

"I doubt there's brains in the whole lot of 'em combined to fathom that one. Your concern is valid though. We'll be long gone before they hit on anything solid. Gentlemen, we best play it close to the vest until this last load is seen to tonight. Until then, I have legitimate cargo to unload. Let us all behave as if nothing were amiss. The Giant knows the schedule. If you see him, please impart our resolve. Luck be with us all."

Back on deck we squinted against the glare of the sun as we disembarked. We took pains to move with distinct though unruffled purpose until we were out of sight of the *Banshee*.

"Good God, Holmes!" said I once we'd rounded the corner of a warehouse. "What manner of cutthroats have we embroiled ourselves amongst?"

"Smugglers for certain," replied Holmes, calmly. "However, this slight glimmer of progress has not brought us closer to the murderer. That is not to say we did not learn much from our performance."

"Who is the Giant?"

"I have no clue."

"I thought we were dead men in that cabin."

"Your concern is justified. We went in on a tenuous bluff but we pulled it off."

"That was all guess work back there?"

"My performance was based on a series of individual conclusions which, collectively, formed a fragile whole. Our inspection of Waters' quarters showed that he was living beyond his means. Conclusion: he had a secondary source of income. The murdered men shared a common past illustrated by the matching tattoos now linked to *Banshee*. Seamen become closer than brothers oftimes, much like soldiers on the battlefield, as you well know. Conclusion: it was unlikely that Waters was lining his pockets without cutting his associates in on the action. It is no coincidence that the murderer struck down only these men. Fact, since Limehouse is a high-crime district, there is a greater police presence thus rendering chance in the selection of three victims, all policemen with past connections, next to impossible and removes the motive of a madman randomly targeting policemen altogether. Captain Lewis has just confirmed that the men were working together and were targeted specifically by the murderer. From this I wove a tapestry that convinced Lewis that the noose was tightening. The threat to one's own mortality breaks down barriers quickly in the mind of the individual. Lewis was no exception and this did half the job of convincing him we were part of the operation and would help him save his own skin while in the act of preserving our own. You'll notice that he trusted us only to a point. He did not name the cargo to be unloaded and deferred to this Giant, whoever that is, to be the one to close this chapter of their operation."

"I see the logic in your reasoning," I conceded. "But if just one of your conclusions had been incorrect...."

"All life worth living involves risk. And we are not done yet. Back to Baker Street for us, Watson. There are preparations to be made."

We headed towards the street in search of a cab.

"That we have uncovered a crime ring is beyond doubt," said I. "What

I cannot fathom is how embroiling ourselves with smugglers will net us a murderer."

"Even at this late stage, you have yet to piece it together," Holmes replied. "You disappoint me, Watson."

To say I was perplexed by the developments and the singular strategy proposed by Holmes would be understatement. That I went along with the wishes of my friend was more a testament to my faith in his abilities than an affirmation of the belief that those abilities were being properly applied to this case.

It was after I had refreshed myself with hearty stew against the chill of the docks that Holmes announced he must depart. I expressed my intention to accompany him—to which Holmes protested, assuring me that he would not be placing himself in harm's way. We hit on the plan whereby I should wait until nightfall then, from a place of concealment, observe the off-loading of *Banshee*'s illicit cargo in order to determine where it was being taken so that word could be delivered to Lestrade.

"Tear a fiver in half," advised Holmes with regards to the logistics of our plan. "Give one half to a cabman with the promise of the other piece only when you discharge him. He will be your man until the last trump."

"And where will you be?"

"I shall be preparing the next part of our investigation. When you have the drop-off point, dispatch one of the Irregulars to the Yard. Once Lestrade and party arrive, slip away and meet me where the body of Morse was discovered. Be certain Lestrade does not learn where you are going and that you are not followed."

"What will you be doing, specifically, while I run about London?"

"Securing a guide, of course," was his cryptic reply. "Check your revolver's load before you head out, Watson. The game's afoot!"

In a display of prudence, I took a roundabout way back to the Limehouse pier once night had fallen. Directing the cabman to overshoot my destination, I was able to approach from the west. I instructed him to halt at the corner of Three Colts Street and Ropemakers' Fields and covered the remaining distance on foot. It was full dark and there was no moon. The fog was thick. However, the persistent breeze off the water kept it from the pier, providing an unobstructed view of the *Banshee*. I was too far away to make out individual faces, but I recognized Captain Lewis from the manner of his dress as he moved about the deck.

One hour's vigil in the damp night air instilled a chill in me which was not dispelled until the *Banshee*'s decks suddenly came alive in the still night. Captain Lewis began waving his arms with distinct purpose. That purpose was demonstrated by the crew who proceeded to lower a gangway and fix ropes to the covering on the cargo hold. Simultaneous to these developments, a large, covered wagon rattled up to the right of my position and came to a halt, horses blowing, before the gently rocking *Banshee*. The cargo hold creaked open and men plunged down into the black maw.

What followed set my teeth grinding together. Ragged, filthy, pitiful, a score of Chinese were herded up on deck with blows and kicks. This despicable scene unfolded in near silence, only adding to the surreal sight before my eyes.

Holmes and I had aligned ourselves with slavers!

The would-be slaves were quickly thrust down the gangway and piled into the rear of the wagon. One of the wretched men abusing the band turned to nod up at Captain Lewis while another had a word with the driver. I sensed an end to this stage of the operation. The wagon would soon be off.

Dashing flat out, I returned to my waiting cab. Righteous indignation in my breast, I barked instructions, then hopped inside and we were underway. Having noted the street the slave wagon had taken on approach to the *Banshee*, I ordered a parallel course and hoped to get ahead of the fiends. As the night was abnormally still, I feared the noise of the cab, even with a block between the two vehicles, might reach the ears of the slavers desperate to avoid detection. Thus it was necessary to outdistance them and lie in wait for their next turn.

A small park with a line of waiting cabs provided the perfect cover and we took up position at the end of the line. Our spot allowed us a view via an alleyway to the street the slave wagon was using and we would see it when it crossed the alley mouth. The canal to the north meant the wagon could go east or west along the water barrier. We lay to the west. If the wagon did not pass us in the next few minutes, then I knew it had gone east and we would resume the pursuit.

The wagon crossed the mouth of the alley. Two minutes crept by and the wagon did not reappear at the intersection up ahead. I thumped the roof of the cab and we pulled out of the queue, turning east. Keeping well back and leaning out the window, I saw the wagon disappear into an abandoned brewery. The doors closed behind it. What fate awaited the unfortunate Chinese I could not hazard a guess. It fell to me to render this point moot.

We halted in a pool of darkness cast by an ancient oak sprawling against the night sky. I climbed down and gave one of Holmes' street urchins precise instructions. The representative of the Baker Street Irregulars had been clinging to the rear of the cab as was his wont and took off like a shot; his destination, the Yard.

I left the cab to get a closer look at the brewery. My revolver in my fist, I inched closer and, through a crack in the warped wall, strained to hear what was transpiring. A veritable Babel of voices met my ears. The wagon was being unloaded, resulting in a lot of chatter and barked orders. However, below that, a discussion was in full heat. The subject of that discussion was the Giant and his whereabouts. It appeared the man was missing and his absence had not been expected. A group of armed men, surly types, made for the door and, supposing a search for the missing man was about to commence, I retreated to a place of relative safety up a darkened side street.

Holmes was expecting me, yet I could not abandon the unfortunate Chinese until I was certain Lestrade had arrived to rescue them. Anxious minutes flew by until, at last, I heard the muffled, stealthy progress of a sizable group drawing closer to the brewery. Whether this was Lestrade and an army of constables or the slavers returning from the search for the Giant, I did not know. Losing myself in a darkened doorway, I watched the group sidle up. It was Lestrade and some twenty police officers, all of whom were armed. I did not reveal myself to them as they passed my hiding place. When they were a short sprint from the place, I heard Lestrade hiss instructions at them.

"Don't shoot unless it's to return fire, lads," he said. "And mind you don't wing Kinney. He's our man in these parts. You can't miss him. He's as tall as an oak. On my signal now."

The Giant was a police officer!

The assault was imminent. Led by the capable Lestrade, I had no doubt of the outcome. By circuitous means I rejoined the cabman and sped off to meet Holmes as the first police whistles shrilled.

Out of the frying pan and into the fire. My cab rolled up on a scuffle taking place. Two men, oddly garbed, moved in and out of the shadows of the deserted courtyard and did not hear the cab pull up.

Launching myself from the cab placed me amidst the scuffling men. A putrid odour emanated from the elder of the two who was clad in a foul, long, greasy velveteen coat, dirty canvas trousers, shoes nothing more than tatters. His fellow combatant was similarly attired, however this man did not reek of a cesspool.

"Assist me, Watson!" shouted the second man a hair's breadth before I recognized him as Sherlock Holmes. "If we lose him, we lose the night!"

I took hold of the man. A good look at his grimy face revealed a man anywhere from sixty to eighty years of age and, for someone of that vintage, he was robust and florid, strong as a bull and slippery as an eel. Twice he almost squirmed loose despite our combined efforts to restrain him. It was the pair of backpacks lying at our feet that finally did him in. The old man's heels became entangled in the strap of one and down he went. My revolver was out before he could recover from his fall. It was cocked and pointed at his head and that settled the matter. The man's shoulders slumped in defeat.

"A wise choice," said Holmes, straightening his peculiar habiliment. "Continue to cooperate and you will be back at your night's work in under an hour. And profit in the meantime. Lash out again and we'll turn your whole crew in. At five pounds a head, it will be I and my associate who stand to profit. Is that clear?"

The old man nodded sullenly. Now that I could see him plainly, my heart sank.

The ratty coat, a canvas apron tied round, a dark lantern similar to a policeman's strapped onto his right breast and, two feet from where he stood glaring at us, a pole eight feet in length, one end of which had a large, iron hoe affixed.

The old man was a tosher.

"Very well," said Holmes to the reluctant nod. "You will guide us where we wish to go and no more funny business."

"Holmes," said I. "There is only one place he can be of any use as a guide."

"True. That is precisely where we are going."

Holmes snatched up one of the bags and held it out to me.

"A trade," he suggested. "The bag and its contents for the gun. Hurry, Watson, time is our enemy."

To the last I could offer no argument. I surrendered my pistol and set about donning my own set of tosher gear whilst I related to Holmes what had transpired at the pier.

"The devils!" said he when I had finished my account. "I knew the extracurricular activities of these corrupt policemen had damned them, but even I did not suspect human slavery! And now this Kinney is part of the group and goes missing. I fear we are too late. Our quarry remains a step ahead but we are gaining ground. Are you ready, dear friend?"

"I am wearing the uniform," I replied. "I cannot say that I am ready for what it represents."

Holmes chuckled. "It shan't be as bad as all that. It shall be much, much worse."

He returned the pistol to my hand, then bent to snatch up and hand the long pole to the old man.

"You've stalled us long enough," said he. "Your associates are no doubt on their way to liberate you. They will not find us here. We'll have your name before we proceed."

"Lanky Bill," growled the old man; toshers were only ever known by nicknames. The breath from his hole of a mouth was as foul as the black stumps of his rotten teeth.

"Lead on, Lanky Bill," directed Holmes.

Our destination: London's sewers.

Toshers made their living by forcing entry into the city's sewers at low tide, searching out and collecting miscellaneous scraps washed down from the streets above. Everything from bones, fragments of rope, scraps of metal, silver cutlery or, if the denizens above were generous in their carelessness, coins of varying denominations swept into the gutters after slipping through the fingers of their owners. The work was not without its hazards and therefore against the law, and Holmes had been quite accurate in his threat as rewards were offered for turning toshers in. This did not deter the class as a veritable fortune was there to be raked in.

Lanky Bill put on another display of strength in prying up the sewer cover and began manhandling it over to one side so we could descend into the mire below.

"How did you hit on the sewers?" asked I of Holmes.

"Elementary," he replied, never taking his eyes off our guide. "Did you not notice that the bodies of Morse and Carter lay very near manholes? Your boot even scraped along one where Carter had lain."

"I made nothing of them," said I as I struggled into the gear. "And what of Waters? Was there a sewer where he was discovered?"

"I do not know. Recall Smythe's account of the werewolf's filthy shoes. The lack of witnesses. The proximity of two sewers to the bodies. Once I realized that the murderer must be using the sewers as a means to move the corpses, it seemed a waste of time to check the location where Waters was found."

"The sewers are fraught with dangers along their labyrinthine length. How did the murderer make his way?"

"The answer is right in front of you," replied Holmes as Lanky Bill had the lead cover sufficiently to one side of the opening. "Isn't that right, old man?"

"I'll not say a word," replied Lanky Bill, sullenly. "You are armed, so I do what I'm told. It's mighty dark down there, mind."

"Try anything," said I, "and your kin will be sifting your bones for the lead I put into you."

"Well said, Watson. To continue: If Lanky Bill is not forthcoming, I shall be so in his place. You may recall I surmised that the murderer must be a man of means or have well-heeled accomplices. I submit that the toshers round here have been enlisted as guides and have been very well compensated for their efforts. And I submit that the murderer has enlisted men to guard any street approach to his lair as a matter of course. If we are to get anywhere, we must circumvent these precautions. What's good for the goose and all that. Lanky Bill will now guide us to the murderer. Is this not so, Bill?"

The grumble from the throat of Lanky Bill answered in the affirmative to all that Holmes had spelled out more than anything the man could have said.

"I shall go first," said Holmes once I finished dressing. "Lanky Bill will follow. Watson, bring up the rear. Quickly now. If we're spotted, we'll all wind up in the clink."

He handed me the revolver.

There were a thousand places I would rather have been at that moment, but there was nothing for it. We descended the slimy steps in that order. The odour assailed the nostrils, making one light-headed. That was only the beginning of the ordeal. Stepping off the ladder, my boots sank ankle-deep into an unspeakable quagmire. We opened the bull's eye of our lanterns and cast feeble light about the loathsome place. We stood amidst a mire of filth comprised of gas works ingredients as well as the wastes from chemical and mineral manufacturers, dead dogs, cats, kittens and rats, offal from the slaughter houses, every manner of dirt from the street pavement above, rotten vegetable matter, stable-dung, pigsty refuse, night-soil, ashes, rotten mortar and any and all manner of rubbish. All of this stretched out in a twisting bilious ribbon in both directions as far along the arched brick tunnel as the eye could see. The chittering of unseen rats everywhere chilled the blood.

"Mind the neighbours, now," said Lanky Bill of the rats. "They'll gang up on us if they get into their heads to. Many a tosher has gone down under the weight of 'em. If any make a move towards ye, use yer pole and strike 'em dead or yer torn to pieces."

I had treated rat bites in the past and they were nasty business. Bites fester, producing a throbbing hard core in the ulcer as big as the eye of a boiled fish which must be cut out after draining. Fifty or a hundred such bites and a man was done for. Worse than this, however, was the threat of death by suffocation or explosion from pockets of gas trapped in the tunnels. Sulphurated hydrogen was the most common and the most deadly. Throw in the risk of disease from coming into contact with all forms of human waste and the need to get our journey over as quickly as possible was self-evident.

"The sluices were raised at low tide," said Holmes, his voice echoing dully off the glistening stones. "This should buy us the time we need to cover the necessary ground."

I had overlooked this new danger. The sluices, one opened, released a tidal wave of effluent-filled water into the tunnels to flush out the system. This filled the tunnels to the ceiling twice daily. Trapped below, one was surely done for; if not dashed to pieces from the wave, drowning was inevitable.

"Let us get on with it, then," I urged.

"You heard the man."

Lanky Bill led the way and we did our best to keep him within arm's length, lest he dash down a side tunnel and leave us to the rats and filth. Our boots sloshed through the waste, stirring up fresh wafts of foulness to make our eyes water and nostrils protest. The tunnel ceiling was a mere four feet from the floor and we stooped to navigate its length, bringing our faces closer to the stink while our backs slid along the ceiling stones picking up all manner of muck. We could barely see three feet in front of us and risked falling with each slippery step on the slimy stones beneath us.

Despite the unsavoury conditions, our progress was steady. Lanky Bill led us with uncanny ability born of long familiarity through the sepulchre gloom. All went as well as could be expected until a series of tiny splashes sounded behind us. These were barely audible over the squelching sounds our boots made as they lifted and fell uncertainly through the shallow water. Holmes recognized the implications of the noise at our rear, a sound of pebbles hitting the water, a fraction of a second before Lanky Bill came to realize it. That split second saved our lives.

Holmes seized the man by the crook of his arm and yanked him backwards so that he was between Holmes and myself.

"They're comin' all right," said Lanky Bill.

I whirled to see a hairy, undulating carpet moving towards us. Rats! Thousands of them. I grasped at once why Holmes wanted the old man where he could see him. Should Lanky Bill have chosen that moment to flee from us, we would be utterly lost dashing headlong up one tunnel or the next in avoiding the carnivorous army at our heels.

"How much farther?" asked Holmes, in a tone of singular calm.

"Fifty yards that way." Lanky Bill jerked a black thumb over his shoulder. His beady eyes were locked upon the approaching rats. The beams from our three lanterns now glittered in the crimson eyes of the first column of the beasts. I fired into their midst; the deafening noise in the confined space gave them pause.

"Run like the devil!" advised Holmes.

For the first fifteen or twenty yards, we kept the rat horde at bay. The fetid water and mud splashed about us as we thrust our feet in and out of it in our mad dash. Then rats began boiling out of a side tunnel as we passed and we had no choice but to fight for our lives. It was here the poles came in handy. The sharp, cutting edge of the hoe attachment made an excellent scythe, cleaving rats cleanly. We did not decimate their ranks but rather slowed their inexorable advance while the vile creatures turned on the injured and slain amongst them.

Holmes put a lit match to the newspaper in his pocket and tossed this torch onto a mound of excrement between us and the beasts. The methane ignited and seared a host of the devils while the group as a whole scrabbled away. This action bought us the freedom we needed to continue our flight.

"That's 'er!" roared Lanky Bill, jabbing a finger at the manholes up ahead. "Not that first! The next!"

Rats began tumbling out of an overhead drain, showering down upon us. We lost precious seconds flinging them from our bodies as they attempted to bite through the layers of our clothing. Meanwhile, the army behind continued its pursuit.

We passed under the first drain Bill had pointed out. Holmes was in the lead.

A second army of rats was closing in from the opposite end of the tunnel. We were surrounded.

"Keep going or we're done for!" yelled Bill, pushing past Holmes to get to the sewer lid. He scrambled up the rusted ladder like a spider up a web and was lunging at the manhole cover as we drew near.

"Run like the devil!"

I was concerned that should Bill get out before us, he might well replace the metal cover and stand on it to ensure our doom under the fangs and claws of the rats, and doubled my speed.

Holmes reached the ladder next. He paused to wait for me as I slid, almost falling.

"Get up there!" I roared. "Or, by God, I'll shoot you!" This was no time to stand on ceremony, although I appreciated the sentiments behind his desire not to leave me behind.

Lanky Bill had the cover loose and scrabbled out. Holmes started up as I reached the bottom rung. The rats were all about me and I kicked savagely at them as I got up on the first step. Climbing like a monkey, I clambered up through the hole. Holmes seized me under the arms and hauled with all his strength. Holmes and I tumbled free and Lanky Bill wasted no time securing the cover. We all three sprawled, panting.

"Nothing like a little exercise to stir the blood, eh?" said Holmes. "Let's catch our breath a moment then be on our way."

"Anyone bitten?" asked I.

It was a miracle that none of us were. Of course our garments had been gnawed into at half a hundred places but toshers habitually dressed in layers for just such and eventuality. We stood. Holmes caught my eye for a moment before turning to Lanky Bill.

"Yer don't need me no more," said Bill. "I want to be shed of you lot."

"And so you shall," said Holmes. "I wanted only to impart my thanks for your efforts during our ordeal."

"I'm truly free to go? You'll not put a bullet in me back?"

"Perish the thought. Yes, we no longer need you. However, we do require your silence."

I was ready, as per the silent communication that had taken place between Holmes and myself, and brought the butt of my revolver down on the back of Lanky Bill's head. The man pitched forward. Holmes caught him and eased him to the stone floor.

"Good show, Watson. I doubt you broke the skin. The headache when he awakens will be another matter. Let's push on, shall we?"

Casting my gaze about in the darkness, I made out only vague shapes. The place was dank, musty, a basement.

"Here is our exit," said Holmes, who had shucked his tosher gear and stood before a short, wooden staircase.

"Where the devil are we?" asked I, shedding my own filthy rags.

"The cellar of an opium den," replied Holmes. "That should be obvious from the smell."

At mention of opium I did detect a faint odour underlying the dust and rot filling my nostrils. How Holmes caught it and instantly identified it was one of the singular abilities I had come to expect from my friend. It was a tremendous relief to be shed of the tosher gear. With a considerably lighter step I joined Holmes at the short staircase, revolver at the ready.

"I suspect, in this instance, that stealth is our ally," said he, nodding at the weapon. "Our quarry has ensconced himself here and engineered his defences to prevent opposition from without. Why else was this interior sewer left unguarded? Well, we have gained entry uncontested. We need only find the man on the premises without being detected. Gunfire will hardly accomplish this end."

I lowered the revolver but remained ready for any eventuality. Holmes gently eased open the cellar door. The intoxicating fumes were overpowering as we stepped into a short, narrow, unlit corridor. Clearly, we were on the other side of one wall of the room upon which so many slaves to the drug travelled on wings of gossamer to who knew what Heaven or Hell. Fortunately, we did not tarry. Holmes spied a rickety staircase to the left and indicated we should proceed in that direction. The door at the top of the stairs was unlocked. With a ginger turn of the nob, Holmes pushed the door open.

The sight that met our eyes did not match our surroundings. Lavish wall tapestries, a crackling fire, subtle incense and a forest of standing candles turned the back room of the opium den into the receiving room of a king's palace. Seated on a simple bench, half if darkness in the far corner of the room, was a robed man.

We stepped into the room and the man came smoothly to his feet.

His features were revealed to us. It was the face of a wolf! I raised my revolver. Holmes stayed my hand.

"That will do us no good."

"What in blazes! This is no mythical beast," said I as I scrutinized the figure. "It is a man."

"I've known that from the first, Watson. Only observe his stance, the readiness, the balance," said Holmes. "Every aspect of the Eastern martial arts. At this distance, the man would be elsewhere before the bullet left the barrel. Though I cannot pinpoint the particular discipline, there is no doubt a distinct Shaolin influence."

We were staring at a man whose face was covered in thick, coarse black hair. Only the eyes and mouth were visible and they were of a benign cast. The hair on his head extended a good eighteen inches from his collar, cascading down onto his chest. My immediate diagnosis was hypertrichosis; an affliction which caused the hair on the body to grow out of control. The fingernails of either hand protruded menacingly, having been grown abnormally long and filed into claws. He did appear, in every aspect, to be the werewolf in the stories the papers had used to terrify London.

"Welcome, honoured gentlemen," said the man in flawless English with the barest hint of the Far East. "I am Mu Kong Tai Djinn."

"Grand Master," said Holmes after we had introduced ourselves. "I sought an audience with you some days ago but was rebuked at every turn."

"Please accept my apologies. My business here could not be delayed."

"The business of murder should always be delayed," said Holmes.

For the first time I saw blood stains on the floor. Glancing around, a rack of weapons on the wall behind the door hinted at the means by which blood had been spilled.

"There is great shame in what I have done," Mu Kong Tai Djinn admitted, lowering his head, "even in righting a terrible wrong."

"Were they your sisters?" asked Holmes. "The victims you avenged."

"I am truly in the presence of one who is worthy," the man said. Grief tugged at the muscles beneath the tufts of long hair. "You are correct. Permit me to tell you the tale. Thinking me a demon due to my condition, my parents abandoned me, still an infant, in the forest where I would have perished. Wandering Shaolin monks came upon me and took me to their temple where I remained under their tutelage and training. My family, having moved away to escape their shame, was lost to me as it grew prosperous. However, my four older sisters had not forgotten their brother and employed agents who got word to me. Against the wishes of my parents, we communicated via an agent, and I learned of their approaching weddings. In my joy, I sought out precious gifts to convey my love as they began new lives. Then the slavers fell upon them one night as they left the marketplace. They were taken, abused, tormented and smuggled aboard a ship bound for England. When the news reached me, I left the temple so that I might free them from their bondage. I traced them here, and learned that their owners had beaten them to death for they would not submit. I was honour-bound to exact justice on the men who did this."

"Watson here has set the police on the slave ring," said Holmes. "They will pay for their crimes."

"The police?" scoffed Mu Kong Tai Djinn. "Those who murdered my sisters wore the uniform of policemen."

"Would you condemn all who wear such uniforms?" asked Holmes. "How different is that from those who brand you, solely on your appearance, as a murdering, soulless monster?"

"You are correct. I beg forgiveness. May I humbly ask if you have turned the slavers over to a man of honour?"

"A man whose integrity is above reproach," said Holmes.

"Excellent. Then my terrible work is complete."

Holmes indicated the bloodstains. "Kinney is dead, then? The Giant?"

Mu Kong Tai Djinn nodded. "He, like the others, received more of a fighting chance than they showed my poor sisters. As Grand Master of Shaolin-Do and master of all skills of the seven temples, I display proficiency with one hundred and forty weapons systems and two hundred different empty hand combat techniques. And so, I allowed each slaver to select the weapon of their choice and to meet me, unarmed, in this room. Honour demanded that I grant them a chance they did not deserve. All were found wanting."

"Kinney's body, then, will be transported through the sewers to be disposed of above?" asked Holmes.

"It is being prepared for transport and unguents are brewing to be used against the rats. I shall carry it personally. It is my burden alone."

"It's cold-blooded murder," said I.

Mu Kong Tai Djinn bowed his head. "I do not deny this. And thus the trail."

"Subtle, yet damning," said Holmes. "I congratulate you."

"You murder these men, then plant the seed of your own destruction. Why?"

"To murder is wrong. It is an evil thing. Yet there is a beast in all of us. It can never fully be purged. When mine is pricked by unholy outrage, I shame myself with those who shamed and destroyed ones dear to me. As penance, I must plant the trail of my doom for one who is worthy to find it. Should that trail be found and followed, I must submit to my fate. It is the only honourable thing to do."

"Then you submit now?" asked I.

"Completely and utterly," replied the Oriental. "I am at your mercy and will offer no resistance. My work here is finished. Justice had been done."

Holmes paused, considering, before he said, "Our work, too, is complete, Grand Master. Come, Watson, let us home."

"That's to be it, then?" said I. "This man killed four policemen...."

"Four heartless murderers dealing in the flesh trade," Holmes corrected. "Watson, we've broken the ring, given the rest of the gang up to Lestrade. The four previous murders have been suitably avenged. And we have solved the mystery. There is no more work for us here. Mu Kong Tai Djinn has left the trail of his guilt with the bodies for Lestrade or any of his fellow detectives to unravel. This affair is finished."

I posed one more question to our host, "What will you do?"

"I shall return home," said he, "and grieve."

Two days later we sat by the fire at Baker Street after having bid farewell to Lestrade who still suffered the woes of Job, though he expressed his relief that no other bodies had turned up. Holmes admitted that there were no avenues of investigation left open to us and he had abandoned the case until such time as new evidence came to light. Lestrade had accepted this.

There were still several aspects of the case which eluded me. I put them to Holmes.

"How did you know it had been his sisters who'd fallen victim to the slavers?"

"The items placed on the bodies. All were feminine accoutrements of disparate styles, which could not match the tastes of any one female: fan, comb, brooch. The only sound conclusion was that the items were for three different women. The bracelet Lestrade just mentioned having been found on the body of Kinney fits this theory. What else troubles you?"

"The significance of the tattoos."

"They were an obstinate variable at first," admitted Holmes. "We have Lestrade to thank for cracking them. He gave us *Banshee* and the merchantmen connection. And from there, the tumblers fell into place. Waters, Morse, Carter and Kinney were growing rich in the traffic of human beings: Asians in particular. To their minds, they had found the proverbial pot of gold. In other words, they had gotten lucky. A corruption of that word in the fractured English spoken by Chinese learning our tongue is 'rucky.' The fiends chose this as their derogatory reminder of their disgusting enterprise. You'll remember that Captain Lewis damned them for it, as it subtly pointed at their guilt."

"This led you to conclude the werewolf was no monster."

"Not right away. The Chinese connotation of the tattoos combined with the murders all taking place in Limehouse with its large Asian population was the first link. The addition of particular Chinese artifacts on the bodies strengthened the connection. The nature of the items told me the murders were not random and most likely committed by someone of Chinese descent. I sought motive. Revenge was one on a considerable list. The slavers you helped bring to justice brought revenge to the forefront. From that moment I knew, without doubt, that our murderer was an avenger. It remained only to track him to his lair so that we might obtain undeniable proof."

These explanations settled my mind on the matter. The day before, Holmes had showed me the notice in one of the papers of a luxury steam yacht of Chinese ownership bound for the Orient, and I did not need his powers of deduction to conclude that Mu Kong Tai Djinn had put England behind him.

"Do you think Lestrade will ever piece the thing together?" asked I.

"We live in an age of miracles, Watson," said Holmes. "Anything is possible. However, I would not hold my breath."

The End

Away from Holmes

Working on tales featuring Sherlock Holmes and Dr. Watson has been a dream come true for me. Although I came late to Doyle's original stories and novels featuring the great detective and the unforgettable Watson, I was soon captivated, as so many readers have been over the years, that I truly began to understand what a privilege it is to write these characters. This in itself has been rewarding and one heck of a lot of fun, but it's not the whole story.

My first Holmes tale won an award, and I've since gone on to write two others that have been very well received (two more award nominations!) and now you've just read my fourth of what I hope will be many more Holmes adventures. Holmes and Watson are now the characters I have written more than any others in my career—and that includes characters I've created. And I'm fine with that.

So why did I leave Holmes?

This past year has been the longest break for me between Holmes tales as it has been the busiest year of my writing career so far. Offers from other publishers as well as opportunities with Airship 27 have kept me pounding the keyboard as if it's going out of style. Meeting deadlines, researching historical periods and having fun along the way, I lost track of time and, before I knew it, I missed Holmes and Watson and couldn't wait to get back to Victorian London to follow on the heels of a new adventure with this dynamic duo. My time away from Holmes made me hungry to sink my teeth into a new tale and here it is. I truly hope you have enjoyed it.

I don't have to tell you how great these characters are. Arguably the most famous fictional characters of all time, how can anyone not enjoy spinning mystery yarns for Holmes to solve? But you've got to make sure you get it right. Doyle rounded out these characters; he set the tone of the world they inhabit. I take it as a personal duty to be true to that in every way possible. There is an essence that must be present in every published Holmes tale or adaptation of the characters. The movies featuring Robert Downey, Jr. get at that heart even though they haven't satisfied every Holmes fan. Sherlock moves the characters into the present day but, again, the truth of who these characters are shines through. And I hope the tale you just finished felt like a Holmes adventure to you.

While writing it, I found some of my recent exposure to the above Holmes adaptations creeping into the style. Added to this was my familiarity with the characters. Both of these elements blurred the lines for me while crafting the tale and I was never sure if the behaviour of Holmes and Watson had been influenced by these recent presentations or if I'd just grown so comfortable with them that they began to take actions and say things of their own volition. Regardless, the tale felt right as I set it down and it was fun work.

I took a different direction with the crime this time out. No spoilers here, but I wanted to tell a Holmes tale that felt authentic, with all of the trappings yet, at the same time, leaned into areas not delved into with the original tales. The villain in the piece was a real man, he did exist, looking as he is depicted in the tale and with the same abilities, and I can only hope I've done him justice in my fictionalized version of someone it would have been an unforgettable experience to meet. As for the crimes under the microscope in the tale, again, I hope they have come across just fresh enough to be engaging while fitting in nicely with the richly detailed world of Victorian London—one of the true stars of any Holmes and Watson adventure.

Well, that's four Holmes tales in the books. Airship 27 is planning a Volume Five and I'm planning to be a part of it. Thanks for reading and let us know what you think of the tales. We write them for you, the fans!

ANDREW SALMON Pulp Factory Award winner and Ellis and multiple Pulp Ark and Pulp Factory Awards nominee Andrew Salmon lives and writes in Vancouver, BC. His work has appeared in numerous magazines, including *Pro Se Presents, Masked Gun Mystery, Storyteller, Parsec, TBT* and *Thirteen Stories.* He also writes reviews for *The Comicshopper* and is creating a superhero serial novel currently running in *A Thousand Faces Magazine.*

He has published or appeared in seventeen books:

The Forty Club (which Midwest Book Reviews calls "a good solid little tale you will definitely carry with you for the rest of your life"), *The Dark Land* ("a straight out science-fiction thriller that fires on all cylinders"— Pulp Fiction Reviews), *The Light Of Men*, which has been called "a book of such immense significance that it is not only meant to be read, but also to be experienced... a work of grim power"—C. Saunders, *Secret Agent X: Volume One* and *Three, Ghost Squad: Rise of the Black Legion* (with Ron Fortier), *Jim Anthony Super Detective Volume One, Sherlock Holmes Volumes One, Two, Three* and *Four, Black Bat Mystery Volume One, Mars McCoy Space Ranger Volume One, Mystery Men (&Women) Volume Two* (with Mark Halegua), *Moon Man Vol. One,* and *The Ruby Files Vol. One* constitute his other work for Airship 27 to date. He has also appeared in *The New Adventures of Thunder Jim Wade Vol. One* from Pulp Obscura.

His work will also appear in forthcoming Airship 27 releases: *Lance Star Space Ranger, Volume Four, Ghost Boy, Volume One, All-Star Pulp Comics #2* as well as the *New Adventures of Major Lacy* and the *New Adventures of Lynn Lash* from Pulp Obscura.

To learn more about his work check out the Airship 27 Hangar at:
http://airship27hangar.com and the following links:
lulu.com/AndrewSalmon and lulu.com/thousand-faces.
amazon.com/Andrew-Salmon/e/B002NS5KR0/ref=sr_ntt_srch_lnk_7?qid=1328666769&sr=1-7
pulpobscura.net/#!

The Mystery of Mr. Holmes

There's a mystery behind Mr. Sherlock Holmes; beyond the canon stories of precise detection and fantastic obfuscation, past the "missing episodes" with which Watson tantalises his readers; further even than the speculations about Holmes' secret months after Reichenbach "under the name of Sigerson".

The character fascinates and resonates. Holmes is analytical and precise in his thinking, he seeks to restore justice, he aids the desperate, yet suffers from character defects of untidiness, rudeness, callousness and antisociability that would usually render him a most unlikeable fellow. He makes it hard for a reader to empathise with him, because the very act of watching Holmes' thought processes destroys the heart of the detective stories in which he features. Yet he continues to inspire and enthral new generations in his original canon, in new literary ventures, in film, on stage, and beyond even that in the wider consciousness of popular culture. Why?

In writing additional Holmes stories the author has to grapple with these questions. If one cannot understand the broad appeal which Holmes satisfies one must at least intuit it enough to offer more of the same.

One key is John Watson M.D. As our usual point-of-view window upon the Great Detective—and indeed often our narrative interpreter of his moods and motives—Watson offers the humanising, compassionate picture that tempers Holmes' otherwise intolerable arrogance. We love and admire Holmes because Watson does.

Another is that Holmes almost inevitably assists those being oppressed by evil against those who would perpetrate it. He's a very devil, but he's our devil, set on against fiends far worse than he who are guilty of crimes far greater than being careless with a slipper full of tobacco or inconsiderate in the matter of late-night violin playing. A kinder, gentler consulting detective would not be so much fun when the game is afoot.

Credit too to Conan Doyle, who quickly identified that Holmes' negative traits could be used in positive ways to keep the character compelling. How much of Holmes' behaviour is eccentric and how much a calculated pose to aid his detection is left to the reader to decide; in fact reading and judging Holmes for oneself is part of the Sherlock reader's experience.

Additional Holmes fiction can too easily pass into pastiche and thence into satire. If we simply invoke the trappings—the pipe, the deerstalker, Lestrade and Jones and Mrs Hudson, the familiar tropes of brougham and country house, the hackneyed phrases of "Remarkable, Holmes!" and "Elementary"—then we miss the heart of Holmes' mystery. More than the furniture of his stories, Sherlock Holmes depends upon the enigma of his own self to address the enigmas laid before him. We depend upon Dr Watson to offer us up the clues to solving Holmes as Holmes solves his cases. A mystery solves the mystery, and readers are invited to ponder both.

It is a privilege for a new writer to be allowed to venture into the mystery and offer another small strand to the tangled affair. Fortunately Holmes can always be counted upon to make the mystery turn out well.

I.A. Watson
Yorkshire, England, 30th December 2009

ALSO AVAILABLE:

Sherlock Holmes:
Consulting Detective

Volume One:

A famous soccer player is found dead in the club house. An unidentified stowaway is murdered aboard a U.S. Navy warship, while another man is found asphyxiated in an empty, locked room. These are several of the twisted puzzles challenging the Baker Street sleuth as he once again takes up the hunt on the fog ridden streets of London accompanied, as always, by his faithful ally, Dr.Watson.

Volume Two:

A twisted scientist plots to alter the course of human evolution while another dreams of creating the world's first mechanical thinking machine. A body is found in a secured bank vault and modern day pirates have begun harassing Her Majesty's Royal Navy. Here are five new mysteries that will test the Great Detective's uncanny talents of observation and the courage of his loyal companion.

Volume Three:

Encounter mythological fairies seeming to plague a beautiful county estate, man-eating tigers on the loose in the streets of London and a stolen museum Mummy. These and other mysteries for intrepid duo of Holmes and Watson to solve!

The game is afoot!

PULP FICTION FOR A NEW GENERATION

NEW PULP

AVAILABLE IN FINE BOOKSTORES WORLDWIDE AND ONLINE OR AT AIRSHIP27HANGAR.COM

ALSO FROM AIRSHIP 27:
The Return of Baron Gruner

In 1902 Sir James Damery enlisted the aid of Sherlock Holmes to prevent the daughter of an old friend from marrying a womanizing Austrian named Adelbert Gruner who was suspected of murdering his first wife. Dr.Watson chronicled the case as "The Adventure of the Illustrious Client." By its conclusion, Gruner's evil intent was exposed to the young lady when Holmes came into possession of an album listing his many amorous conquests. A former prostitute mistress of the Baron's then took her own revenge by throwing acid in his face – permanently disfiguring him.

Holmes believed the matter concluded. He is proven wrong when a hideous murder occurs rife with evidence indicating the Baron has returned. Soon the Great Detective will learn he has been targeted for revenge in a cruel and sadistic fashion. Not only does the Baron wish his death but he is obsessed with causing Holmes emotional suffering. He desires nothing less that the complete and utter destruction of the Great Detective in body and soul.

Gary Lovisi spins a fast paced tale of horror and intrigue that is both suspenseful and poignant, all the while remaining true to Arthur Conan Doyle's original stories. "The Baron's Revenge" is a thrilling sequel to a classic Holmes adventure fans will soon be applauding.

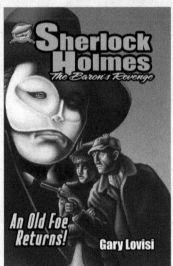

Sherlock Holmes
The Baron's Revenge

An Old Foe Returns!

Gary Lovisi

AN AIRSHIP 27 PRODUCTION

NEW PULP

PULP FICTION FOR A NEW GENERATION
AVAILABLE AT AMAZON.COM AND AIRSHIP27HANGAR.COM

CPSIA information can be obtained
at www.ICGtesting.com
Printed in the USA
FSHW020503260221
78973FS

9 780615 758237